UNDERSTANDING ALMOST NOTHING OF THE WORLD

Spineless Wonders
ABN98156041888
PO Box 220 STRAWBERRY HILLS
New South Wales, Australia, 2012
www.shortaustralianstories.com.au

First published by Spineless Wonders 2020

Typeset in Adobe Garamond Pro

National Library of Australia
Understanding Almost Nothing of the World /James Hughes

ISBN978-1-925052-78-7
A823.4

A catalogue record for this
book is available from the
National Library of Australia

This project has been assisted by the Copyright Agency Cultural Fund.

COPYRIGHTAGENCY
CULTURAL FUND

UNDERSTANDING ALMOST NOTHING OF THE WORLD

JAMES HUGHES

Contents

Nightshift n' Nightingale

As a kid I was ashamed of my younger sister's clustery, carroty freckles. I saw her face as an affront: a distorted reflection of my own. If I saw her in school, I turned the other way. If she had the nerve to sit close on the bus, I found another seat.

This went on, and on and on.

She had a ritual. Every night she rocked back and forth on pillows up against the wall at her back. Bumping, she called it. The nocturnal, muffled sound of my sister's bumping became routine as the sound of my own breathing.

When my sister bumped, she sang. One called up the other, and one was incomplete without the other. How she did both simultaneously she alone knows.

The bumping and singing, on reflection, were sounds of someone smothering unhappiness.

Not that all her songs were troubled or perplexed. There were joyous, free-spirited, wandering songs.

Some songs had no words, only shades of feeling. Sometimes these strange expressions of the soul suddenly turned up a word, then another, finding refrain, morphing to mysterious mantra, into sleepy incantation.

Songs circled. Songs changed emotional horses, mid-stream. Songs fizzled.

Longer compositions always drifted into interlude. The singing softened, dissolved, leaving only tempered bumping – then returned with wings as if wherever she'd gone in her thoughts she'd met something emboldening.

The gumball machine always seemed to me to belong in another girl's bedroom. The gumballs, like so many shades of unblemished happiness, were too simple for someone so problematic.

The machine developed its own complication. The metal twist-latch that released the sweets became hopelessly jammed – nobody could fix it, not even Arthur Lovett next door. In his gravelly emphysema voice he told my dad, 'Tricky glitch, that. Don't like conceding defeat Bill, but it beats the shit out of me.'

Buried deep in the garden I found an instruction manual written in a tongue only I could decipher; half Egyptian half Japanese, revealing the machine's inner secrets. In the dream I fixed the machine. In the dream I was a friend to my sister.

The summer our dad took a nightshift in a dairy, he took to drinking a bit too often in the afternoons. He drank with a friend, now shift-partner, who had arranged the job.

Gerhart Gunter lived three doors up on the opposite side of the street. Bullish and fun-loving, with a thick black beard and animated accent, he was often extending and embellishing his family home with his own hands and tools. One year he'd even made a hammock from scratch, as a wedding-anniversary gift to his wife. In the Gunter's above-ground pool we kids made rocking whirlpools, hauling circles until we were leaden-legged chanting *Whirrrrrlpooool, Whirrrrrrlpooool* as twigs and leaves and always the odd beetle needing rescuing pooled swept along.

Gunter also brewed his own moonshine. Somebody dubbed it white-lightning. The clear, harmless-looking fluid meted from the tiny penis of a porcelain boy in braces and knee-length shorts unzipped, grinning atop Gunter's games-room bar.

All the men in our street had sampled Gerhart Gunter's white-lightning.

Once was enough, for most.

Walking home from school one sticky, unusually sullen afternoon, I was making a song and dance of keeping a distance from my sister. She was dragging her feet so that I might bridge the gap, so that we might meet, maybe even chat. I actually stopped cold to prevent going closer.

Turning the air blue I steamed right past her.

The pebbles in the drive crunched. From the lounge-room carried the voice of boring old Elvis. Elvis on the record player meant my dad had been up at Gunter's. His face soured at the window, seeing me at the gate. I loosened the bolt.

'Keep that gate locked.' He stood at the flyscreen.

'Why?'

'Because I –' A hiccup made mockery of the tone he sought. '- bloody well said so.'

Casually I disobeyed and said something about my sister only having to open it again. I heard the soft crunch of her sandals on the pebbles.

On the veranda I kicked off shoes, opened the flywire. His strange mood was suddenly tangible – as if he was breathing something malignant. A woozy stench of white lighting lingered. He looked like a stranger stranded somewhere he barely recognized. He blocked my way in or maybe I blocked his way out. I went around. My sister brushed past him.

'Excuse me,' he objected, 'excuse me is what you say when you push past like a –.'

She stared. 'I didn't.'

'Are you calling me a liar?'

'You were in the way.'

He followed me into the kitchen with a low, forced laugh. 'I'm in the way?'

The sound of her closing her bedroom door carried to the kitchen. I stood looking into the fridge, deciding what to eat. He was standing behind me. I felt his sustained scrutiny. I pretended, at first, not to notice. Then I switched to projected indifference, deliberately letting him know that his disapproval couldn't touch me.

'And who are you to be walking in here with that standoffish superior scowl?'

I closed the fridge door, forgetting what I wanted, and stood at the sink with back turned again.

'The girls in your class must swoon at that all that charm.' He made a strange, mocking sound. 'Then again…'

From the dish rack I picked up one of the IXL jam-jar glasses.

'Thirteen and you've the face of a bloody hanging judge.'

'Fourteen.' With an uneasy hand I filled the glass and drank. From the lounge, someone in the crowd called something to Elvis, bringing Elvis to briefest laughter, bringing on a wave of adoring laughter.

My dad turned away. The slatted sliding door dividing kitchen and lounge rattled as he shut it.

In the lounge he swore under his breath – out of Benson & Hedges. Any minute he'd open the dividing door, ask me to nip down the milk-bar and keep the change.

Before I'd had a chance to weigh the satisfaction of refusing him against the satisfaction a pineapple donut offered, the door reopened.

'What makes you such a self-important little so and so?'

I turned to leave. He took a step, blocked me. I gave an uncertain push with a shoulder. 'Least I'm not drunk.'

'Well I may have had a couple of drinks up the road, but with a mug like yours, boyo, I'm –'

My other shoulder met him with more force. When I used the shoulder again he met it with a little force of his own. Something in me panicked – I flung out a flimsy left fist. He caught it like a ball tossed in play, twisted down, so I was forced to rotate – like we were in an ungainly dance. A muddled, hurt look in in his eyes told me he didn't know how we'd come to this either. By nature he was gentle.

I was in no physical pain but as our hands unclamped I let out a yowl.

I burst into the bedroom.

My breaths were tight. On the wooden sill by the flyscreen a moribund moth expired with a last half flap. Outside was all glower and glare, as if the air itself had no sympathy.

The longer I stood stewing the more I welcomed the development. Part of me was pleased – now I had full license to refuse all discipline, all tact.

I swivelled at the sound of the door opening. The door hadn't been touched. It was her door. I put knees to the bunk and an ear to the wall.

Something rattled.

'Don't drop it,' she said, firm.

He said something defensive and muddled.

Now I stood in her doorway. He held the gumball machine upside-down, clutching it at the base, insisting in a strange, defiant tone that he could fix it, that he didn't appreciate her running him down. In confusions he lunged to take it back. He swung it upwards, like a stick raised too high for a dog's leap, and lost his grip – the airborne contraption was vertical a moment then flipped, dropping head-first, thumping her dresser and breaking, disgorging its colourful insides to the carpet in rattling cascade. He called after her but she was already out the front door and down the veranda.

A moment later I was out the down the veranda going after her.

The road was abrasive in socks. She looked over a shoulder and ran harder. Just as if I'd picked it up and thrown it myself, I could feel the gumball-machine on my palms and fingers. All of this – all of it – was my fault.

She ran across Waratah and she leapt the ditch and parted two strands in the wire fence and wriggled through. When she was angry her strength and stamina were uncanny.

I followed through the wire fence. In the field she ran much faster. A slate-blue cloud in the shape of a tornado hung motionless on the other side of the fields. For one moment she appeared to be running to meet it. Thirsting forgiveness, I hounded her.

I reined her in, eventually.

She panted, exhausted, for now. 'Get lost.'

'Just – let me be your friend.' I felt as if I oozed slime.

I chased again – she deviated and veered indiscriminately like someone trying to shake a wasp.

When I next came close we were a long way from anywhere. The cloud we were moving toward didn't look like a tornado anymore, only an apostrophe.

She swivelled and shouted. 'Why doesn't our family love each other?'

'Don't say that.'

'Mum and I are the only ones who know what love is. When she's not home it's like I'm a germ.'

'You're my sister – don't say that.'

'*Sister*,' she hissed as if the word were a curse.

Our soles flattened the grass, in stride. Our breathing regulated, restored, a few steps at a time. Afraid to go to her side in case she ran again, I settled for two steps behind.

She said, in odd, methodical rhythm, each word distilled, 'Mum and I love enough for us all but we can't be the *only ones*, it's time for the rest of you to *learn to feel love*.'

A brown horse looked up from grazing, fifty feet away. I'd been so anxious to absolve myself, I'd missed it completely. So had she, judging by her abruptly uncertain steps. The horse watched her shy, hopeful approach. Something about the flies circling its drowsy tail reminded me it was my night to feed the cats.

With a snort the horse swung away in trot, its two-tone brown and black tail bobbing on its smoothly muscular buttocks. As it moved into canter, tremors from its hooves carried underground. My sister was chasing a horse – surging after it as if its running away from her was the last straw. I changed course, walking in the direction she'd run. The scraggly smell of the horse's mane hung back.

The horse curved into the distance, using its easy momentum. She gave up the chase, forked the other way. I jogged, to be with her. She blazed away from me, again.

By the time we were close again I had a double-stitch. My fingers interlocked over my crown as I sucked down air.

She said, 'Dad never wanted us.'

'Don't say serious things.'

'I heard him.'

Our soles landed, step upon step, on tougher grass.

'I heard him say it. He said *I only ever wanted one.*'

I was silent three, four steps. 'When?'

'When *what?*'

'When did he say it?'

'Why does it matter when?'

I swallowed air. 'What did mum say?'

'She was . . . just sort of . . . quiet a long time.'

We walked on. A small family of pines materialized ahead. She saw them and instinctively adjusted her line, just as I did.

I ducked through a quiver of gnats. 'Then what?'

She watched the grass flattening underfoot. 'Then ... I don't know what. Then I went back to bed. I'm not an eavesdropper. I just heard it . . . by accident.'

Something in her voice, maybe her having resigned to its being true, just did something to me. Somewhere in me a knot unwound. Something released from wherever feelings hide and dwell. It swam for surface then held up, tight in my throat.

'Why does he drink that stuff?' She made a face and the flesh between her eyes scrunched. 'Just because it makes him feel like singing?'

A teasing raindrop dived between us with a whisper.

She looked at me for an answer. 'Why doesn't he just sing when he feels like singing? Anyone can sing whenever they want.'

We gravitated toward the pines. One was lopsided and shorter than the others and raised two fists.

She glowered looking down, like she'd remembered something even more bemusing.

I was still afraid she'd reignite – afraid she'd lump me in with dad if she told mum, when mum got home from work, tonight.

A night we were altogether in the lounge, mum showed us a lot of old photos of times they were young in Ireland. One picture was twice the size of all the others. In the picture my dad soft-shoed across a stage, flanked by guys with shiny quiffs, absorbed in playing guitars. Holding the microphone as if it was a very easy, natural thing to be doing, like he was just following an irresistible impulse to sing and dance, my dad beamed.

Mum told us his band had been called Coda Decoders. The name made me howl, just howl at the ceiling. I asked him what he'd been singing when the picture was taken. He was sitting in the brown leather chair by the window, reading *The Herald*. The pages agitated. He said he couldn't possibly remember. He said he'd only ever sung other people's songs. My sister asked how come he hadn't just made up his own. The mildly annoyed, mellifluous voice behind the newspaper said he supposed he didn't have the talent.

She stared at the pages held high like a shield.

In the corner the heater's silver grate gave a metallic *pinnnngggg*, reverberating.

She asked him how someone could tell, if they had talent, or not.

When she was sixteen, my sister took her first singing lessons. Saturday mornings, in our brother's chocolate-brown Falcon, I'd drive her to the teacher's house, park somewhere quiet to read for about an hour, and drive us home again.

On the way there one morning, to our surprise, I asked her what kinds of things the teacher said, in a typical lesson. She said that in last week's lesson she'd been learning how to breathe. I said I didn't see how anyone could concentrate on breathing while singing. With a quizzical half smile, she suggested maybe that was why it had to be taught. I stared ahead. In the brown steering wheel's moulded grooves my fingers had the faux nonchalance of the recently licensed.

She asked what it was like working in a fibreglass factory with dad. I shrugged as if my direction wasn't my doing, or even my concern. After two weeks wandering around university I'd quit without distress, without inkling it might be me and not the university that left something to be desired.

About the factory, there wasn't much to share: brain-shrinking repetition; chemical fumes; mixing and lugging endless buckets of vaporous green resin to roll onto raw fibreglass sheets; clock hands on a go-slow between seven and eight, as if they too dreaded the ten-hour haul. Initially I'd told myself it was only until I had enough money for a car. Then I was telling myself it was to save for university next year. Without even realizing I'd started a needless, rudderless, stupidly unrelenting long-distance run from asking: where do I belong?

The Falcon rumbled accelerating. In a field by the vineyards, a platinum horse grazed, swishing a dirty-white tail. My sister asked how come I never saw my friends now. I watched the road, feigned inattention.

She repeated herself.

I gave a look as if the question was inane – as if she had no place questioning a figure of my standing.

She hesitated. 'Just because your pride's hurt doesn't mean you can't see your friends.'

'Who said my pride's hurt?' The blasé tone bombed.

'It's not a crime to have bruised pride, Patrick.'

'I'm aware, but I don't, so why keep saying it?'

'It's happened to me about a hundred times. It's happened to most people lots of times.' She watched the road, unsure she should wade deeper. 'It's just … Life, having your pride broken over and over,' receding a little into the seat, 'doing your best to fix it up again.'

As a bedside alarm in his first nightshift year, my dad used a clock-radio tuned to bygone sounds. I remember two songs – each heard once and never again. One rattled by with snappy snare and jazzy trumpet and sassy quips about a noisy milkman. *Stop that A-Grade Riot / Keep those bottles quiet.* I remember thinking it uncanny, his hearing that as he got up at midnight to go to a dairy. *So keep those bottles quiet / Cut out or lullaby it.* The song came and went in two, maybe two and a half minutes.

The other seemed to have no beginning or end. Its serenading woke me – a syrupy, lovelorn voice seeping into every room. I could hear dad moving around in their bedroom and couldn't understand why he didn't turn it off. I remember feeling angry for my mum – wishing she didn't have to hear it.

And I remember wishing he didn't have to leave us this late.

I remember him moving around, as if he was looking for something he'd mislaid. The mooning, oddly directionless song seemed to be adding to his confusion, preventing him finding whatever he'd lost. I remember ignoring a voice in my head telling me to go to him and help him look.

The singer seemed to languish somewhere outside time. Amplified by sporadic static at moments it reared up hissing insisting on being heard.

The longer I listened, the more riveted and repelled I was by its swooning reminiscing. Behind the pining was something self-adoring – something feigning feeling: a trickster.

As if it sensed and resented my resistance, suddenly the voice made itself bigger than the house. Something rushed all my circuits – this pure love for my family. The sensation was unlike anything I'd ever felt. Every nerve tingled – as if I'd gulped of a mysterious potion. All my blood flooded with a wish to protect my family. The voice laughed with all it had – a jolt of panic sat me upright. Seamlessly the song resumed. I prickled all over – I knew what I'd heard. I knew what I'd heard but couldn't be certain.

The Stone, The Storm, The End of Huckleberry Finn

Clearing my mother's shed recently I stumbled on a stray pack of Polaroids. I found my brother, sister and I in the bruise-blue ocean one Easter Sunday: Leo slender as a fawn, bending, cupping the froth; Sinead in board-shorts, watching him, bemused; me charging an oncoming wave. The kind of photograph only a mother's lens could orchestrate.

I nearly missed him, closer to camera on the wet sand.

Ears pegged back, front paw cocked, crooked tail afloat.

Our first dog was gaunt and tan with a sleepy pungent fart that made my sister cackle and my dad wince and frown over *The Herald*.

The days we were a family had him at their fragile axis.

When he leant out of our sunburnt station-wagon his liquorice lips flapped and downy ears folded back revealing smoothly grey bulbs, and a tunnel that could only have led to his gallant soul. I imagined climbing through, becoming part of him.

My old man was short with a sturdy veneer and a gorgeous deep doomed laugh, a holder of the floor at barbecues and neighbourhood New Year's Eve parties; always making other men laugh, shaking a match in blue-grey fog.

At home he was always shaking his head, inventing reasons things couldn't be achieved.

Late on the fourth night the dog was missing I stood behind the lounge room door and heard my mum accuse him of driving the dog away – of leaving him on the side of a road, to appease an old neighbour complaining about his midnight moon songs.

'Never mind the happiness of your own children and family. So long as the neighbours aren't inconvenienced … God forbid.' She sounded afraid of her own words. 'Isn't that what's happened?'

I pictured him staring out the blackened window.

She repeated the question.

He struck a match, returned the box to the coffee-table's glass top, said she was as mad as her sister had ever been.

'Why won't you just admit what it is you've done?'

'And why won't you just bloody-well leave me in peace?'

'You're planning to go?' Her words lit a flare of fear in me. 'Is that why you're doing this? This is your way of preparing us?'

'*Theresa.*' He flipped ash into the heavy, octagon ashtray. 'I did not *touch* that dog.'

'You haven't even the – why did you even have a family ... if you didn't want a family . . . to love?'

Seven days and nights after the dog had disappeared, my brother and sister and I burst open the car-doors as mum turned the station-wagon into the driveway – the dog thrashed its tail, spinning circles behind the gate! Dad was standing on the veranda smoking, wearing sunglasses. The dog was emaciated but he was alive and seconds later we were soaring at his side charging to the windy park singing his name for the whole neighbourhood.

We never found out where he'd been, how he'd gotten home.

In a less chaotic world the animal's tribulations would have ended there.

Fate dealt an even stranger hand, a year later.

My family has never talked about it.

She appeared one Sunday stuffing junk mail in letter-boxes. (*I FOUND it at FOSSEYS!*) Her harried walk looked out of step with the lilting late afternoon.

As she lifted the letterbox lid the dog nipped the back of her hand. My mother put the hose down by the geraniums – apologizing at once, asking her inside.

'What and get savaged a second time?'

'Please ... if you're hurt?'

'Some of us have to work.' She traipsed to the Lovett's letterbox.

I'd seen her before. On the other side of the neigh-bourhood, where I walked from the bus-stop, I'd see her going up her doorstep lugging a plastic laundry basket spilling over with crumpled shirts and school uniforms. A prison-grey front wall stood over a lifeless yard, where even the scanty grass seemed begrudged. By the kerb, nailed to a knee-high stake, the lid of an ice-cream container advertised

Ironing Done Here

Reasonable Rate

She decided to sue.

My brother and sister and I knew nothing of this development, at first.

Suing for compensation was just becoming a bit of a thing in 1985 Australia. My family were hardly fertile ground. My mum worked in a paint shop. (*Bristol Colours Your World!*) My dad had just started the night-shift in a dairy, with a neighbour, after being retrenched as a salesman for a greeting-card company. (He'd told his own father across the oceans he was doing a 'night-time operational pasteurisation filtration course.')

As a kid I had this habit: I'd stand in the hall, clandestine, listening to my parents slashing each other with words the way only the Irish can. I knew it was wrong. But I also knew about his affair, and things to do with money.

This time they weren't exactly arguing but something was seriously secretly wrong.

'She's going for our throats, Theresa.' He inhaled Super Mild. 'The bitch has us over a bloody barrel.'

'I could ring Gran . . . she'd lend us enough for a solicitor.'

He drew deeper on the cigarette. 'I've a feeling we've exhausted that option.'

'Thanks to your –' She censored herself, seemed to look away.

'Thanks to my what?'

I felt him scowling at her; felt him look away at the darkened window.

I kept still, staring at the strip of light between the door's bottom edge and the carpet.

Our grandmother's clock went *tlinnng*, ten times, the short-lived silences between notes encapsulating time's mystique.

He said something low and grave. I leant closer.

'I couldn't.' Terrific sadness filled her voice. 'I will not to do that to these children.'

'We might have to, Theresa.' He stubbed his cigarette. 'If that's the only way she'll agree not to try for a pound of flesh . . . we might have to.'

'We can't *allow* a *stranger* do as she pleases with our lives – with our children's lives.'

'And would you prefer to be dragged through some court and end up owing her a big bag of money we don't have?'

My breaths tightened.

In bed I lay awake. The dog slept at my feet, bamboozled by a dream.

At the end of the next school day I was surprised at the sight of the Mazda parked by the school-bus bays. Dad saw me coming, and touched between the lenses of his Polaroids. I went for the front seat and he told me to save it for my sister. When I asked what he was doing here he said he just felt like saving us the drudge of the bus on such a muggy day.

Leo showed up dehydrated and drained after a hard day taunting teachers.

Our sister approached hunched under the weight of her bag. Dad started the car.

She took the front and he leant to give her a kiss and the prickles of his beard touched her soft, freckly cheek. As we spluttered out the school gates she asked why the dog hadn't come for the ride.

He stared at the road as if he'd not heard.

She asked could we take him down the beach after tea, if it stayed this hot. His head kind of titled away from the question. Plumes of cigarette smoke expelled from his nostrils, sucked out the open window.

On the highway, hairdryer-hot air whipped through all four windows and pooled in flux. My sister leant out her window and her hair fanned like wildfire.

Stopped at the lights outside the Technical School, the ABC radio newsreader forecast a change with the chance of a storm. Silence filled the airwaves a moment, as if he were giving listeners time to absorb the information.

On the veranda we kicked off our shoes.

Dad asked us to come into the lounge, altogether.

'Why?' Leo peeled sweaty socks. 'Did we win Tatts?'

Dad closed the flywire, stood staring, distractedly, at a square of sun on the carpet, by the stained glass strip at the front door.

In the lounge we stood between the TV and coffee-table. He squatted, was silent a moment, said he had something to tell us.

He began with hesitation, stumbling on the words. Then he told us. And then the words became meaning-less and soundless. My brother roared, left the room, pushed open the flywire and slammed the gate going out. My sister shook her head, not feeling the hands holding her shoulders, refusing the nonsensical, alien words.

In my own ears came a dull ringing.

'Let me get this straight ... because it sounds so fucken piss-weak I can't believe it.' Ronnie Roscoe had one sole on the kerb and one on the baking bitumen. 'She sent a letter saying she was setting up some two-bit pie-in-the-sky court case – now Huck's pushing up daisies.' He scratched a nipple. 'They backed down to an ironing lady.'

Beside me on the kerb Leo blushed, staring at the bitumen in stoniest shame.

Roscoe shifted his weight, foot-to-foot. 'Someone should pay her house a visit with a can of spray paint.'

Nobody answered.

Roscoe bristled. 'What, so sitting here dying in the arse is better?'

Leo stood, gave his best friend a pissed-off look.

'Good old Huck.' Ronnie Roscoe kept shaking his head. 'What an absolutely piss-poor way to go out.'

On the bottom-bunk in a broiling bedroom I disowned thoughts of the dog, dwelling instead on the minutiae we turn to when we ache: a brittle, spindly wire in the light globe like a static stick-insect stuck in a jar; a scorch in the bunk's grain like the tapering beak and head of a misshapen bird; a patch of carpet glowing and dulling with the sun's on-again off-again pulse.

I felt the dog's name in my guts. Felt it rise, constrict in my throat. For a half moment, just a dizzy blink in time, I felt that I had only ever imagined him. A memory came and I smothered it. Another came and I banished it, too. The dull ringing in my ears resumed and came as relief now – ruling a line through feeling.

I pictured going to the woman's house, in the dark, armed with a stone.

I saw myself, standing in the barren garden; saw myself taking close-range aim, at the window. The stone propelled end over end. The window shattered inward. Saw her run into the room seeing the carpet covered in shards. Saw myself standing there, brazen, brave, belligerent.

Staring at the ceiling, watching the seething fantasy playing on repeat, curious cadences came to me. *Stone in the hand, stone in the hand, stone in the hand. Sole against road, soul against road. They began to mesh. Sold for stone, stone for the road, soul for the stone . . .*

I left the room.

From the fence inside the gate I took up the bike.

On the road outside her house I rolled circles. My spokes ticked, ticked.

At the edge of her yard a new water-metre protruded, salubrious slate-blue like a submarine's surfaced eye.

A neighbour's front garden was colourful and abundant.

On her other side, was a permanently unused block where no birds ever came. In its heart a thorny, impenetrable looking thicket hunched. I found myself listlessly gazing into the strangely lifeless block, as if waiting for something to show up there.

In the corner of an eye I caught a twitch in the blind at the woman's window – one of my arms reacted with a little zapped sensation, like I'd touched an electric fence.

I went rolling downhill, a coward.

I took a right along unpaved Ruth Road feeling the ripples and ridges shake the frame all the way into my backbone. 'Spine,' I murmured, three times.

I found myself about a mile from home, pulled up where the mini-bike racing track had once been; a place I'd forgotten. A stone's throw away, where the finishing line had been, a kid in a pink Hot Tuna singlet lost ground in tug-of-war with a dog wresting a stick. Somewhere behind me a crow went *ha-haaa … haaaaar*.

In the grass by the bike's front wheel, a broken brown shoelace lay like an earthworm halved by a spade. A kinked can of SOLO half submerged showed only the SO. Ants ferried an upturned Christmas beetle still kicking. I scanned for a twig, something to prod the beetle free. A mottled, withered leaf just beside me would do the trick. I bent to pick it. Something whacked my left ear – I threw out an arm and covered up and dropped the bike and grazed a shin leaping the frame all in one move. The magpie swung a U, took cold-eyed aim for a fresh swoop. I ran a messy S and backtracked and yanked the handlebars and kicked away flooding adrenalin.

Cutlery did most of the talking at the table. We all avoided each other's eyes. Dad cleared his throat a few times, as if it explained things. Mum tried a few times to talk about other things. But each of her words required strength and artifice. She'd made a terrible mistake and knew it.

Leo's chair legs scraped the kitchen floor as he stood, leaving the wishbone to one side of his plate.

The screen-door closed limply behind him. The gate opened and the sound of his steps down the gravel carried.

I glanced at my dad. Something in the simple sound of his eating suddenly riled me. I resented his eating – resented his *being*. In his face I saw none of my own. In his cowardice I saw none of my own.

Alone in the twilit garden I went on awhile as if nothing had happened – resuming a private never-ending cricket tournament between imaginary nations: Zulu Lowlands, New Caledonia Highlands, United Regions of Eastern Nowhere and Arctic Archipelago.

When I came around the back of the house looking for a wayward ball, I came across his water bowl. A baby mosquito floated face down in a placid, lukewarm lake.

I carried the bowl to the compost.

I put my nose to the edge of the bowl and caught his animal scent and felt his soul flare and pulse in me somewhere deep. In the compost, watermelon rinds crawled with ants. I emptied the water with a sloppy splash – gnats rose, startled, from the stink. Between the compost and back fence, the idle incinerator gave off its strange scorched whiff. For a moment its pale grey concrete was a featureless face silently commiserating. I pressed a palm to its warmth. I held it there.

I pictured the pale grey concrete wall over the woman's window. *Stone in the hand, stone in the hand.*

Cicadas piped up. At first, each was distinguishable, different in its pitch.

In the dusk a silhouetted sparrow cut twitchy diagrams like blackboard equations. The strangest thought insinuated itself – nothing mattered. It had happened and now couldn't be made right and now nothing mattered. A more familiar, associated thought reintroduced itself: God was make-believe. He was made up. Nothing mattered. They were lonely thoughts and I didn't want them. But they'd come to me without my asking and what could you do about a thought happening?

Mosquitoes attacked.

Dark claimed the dusk.

In bed I lay frozen. I hadn't done my maths homework, again – maybe the three of us would get a day off school, as consolation … console . . . consternation … consecration . . . words blended and blurred, hovered, in and out of reach . . . conjure . . . con . . . sold soul . . . soles in the road . . . *stone in hand* . . . *stone in hand* . . .

Each time Leo turned to his other side the top bunk squeaked, rocked a little.

Across the road a sprinkler ticked, hissing each turn.

'Where do you reckon his spirit went?'

His reply was ghostly, forever coming. 'Who knows.'

My stomach lifted, lowered, every breath.

'What do they do with his body?'

The bunk squeaked, creaked.

The sprinkler ticked, twitched.

He murmured, 'How should I know.'

I stared at the ceiling. I could almost feel the stone.

Through the wall, came the singing. Every night, our sister sang herself to sleep. Tonight, the sorrowful sound froze me, filled me with tender dread … I wanted to comfort her. Something prevented me.

Something always prevented me.

My sister slept. My brother slept. My drowsy mind's eye threw up words like bits of ill-matched jigsaw adrift. Stone … soul-bone … wishbone closing …soul-closing storm bones … I stood at the woman's window, close as I could get my face to the glass. Dad shared her bed. In a coffin by the bed lay my sister. The splayed dog had been nailed to the wall.

I woke and stared at the dark ceiling.

The flyscreen frame trembled, chattered.

A surge of wind blew over the house like a bloated, heaving, waterless wave. My body was hoisted from bed.

Standing at the bedroom window I peered into the dark. Standing on the nature-strip, by the drive, my dad waited for Gerhart Gunter's truck. A gust laid bare his bald patch and I felt this stab of unexpected love. I wanted to call out something, but couldn't think what to say.

Something prevented me.

He cupped his hands and tried to light a cigarette but the spark in his lighter was gone. His hands slid inside his pockets, and he gave the nature-strip a resigned little kick. In profile, staring down at the grass, his nose made me think of a beak, a hawk...

The wind muttered, bumped into things.

The chattering sprinkler made full pirouette.

His hands whipped out of his pockets as Gunter's truck started and backed from his drive. I listened to the truck idling, paused on the road outside his house. I pictured Gunter tuning the radio or leaning across the seat rifling in the glovebox. The engine gave a sudden impatient roar and Gunter was at my dad's side. The door handle gave a clank as my dad opened and Gunter's radio filled the night.

for an UPtown Girl
she's my UPtown Girrrrrl
You know I'm in love with an –

He shut the door with the truck in motion again. They leaned around the corner, picked up speed along Ikara, slowed again at the corner of Moonah, and with a muffled roar were gone to another world.

The wind mumbled.

The wind spoke a hissing, inciting, secretive tongue. Words swished around my head, like bits of broken off dream. Embark … embed … embedded in bed … emblaze …

On the carpet I found crumpled shorts.

The flyscreen's clumsy weight and width caused me to lose grip. The thwack of metal edge on carpet was enough to break Leo's snoring. The bunk squeaked, as he rolled over. *Wake him and go together. Get him to throw the stone. Go alone. Get back in bed. Go tomorrow.*

Go tomorrow, tomorrow.

Outside, the night flew into a rage. The warm breath of something huge found its way in, raising the fur on both my forearms.

And now I was squirming through the cavity between extended window and wooden sill, wriggling like something hatching impatient for life. Misjudging the easy drop to the flowerbed I crash-landed – the window frame shuddered.

I crept around the front of the car. The gravel underfoot made me picture rosary beads.

From under the unloved bush in the corner of the driveway I chose a stone the size of an egg, shinier and imbued with more power, I fancied, than any of its companions – as if it had chosen me. I tiptoed down the rosary-beads. *Hail Mary full of grace … the Lord is with thee.* On the bitumen I stopped, balanced on one leg then the other, brushing pebbles from the arches of my feet, from between toes.

Now the wind swept me into its current.

The smell of rain rode the wind.

The warm bitumen was alive with barefoot nuance.

Ragged clouds scudded. The moon appeared to be on a wild voyage running the other way. A raindrop spattered the road, wetting my toes, then another and another. I smelt the dust on the road, I smelt the dust on the road, I smelt the dust on the road. I have a stone in my hand … I have a stone in my hand. I am brave, I am brave … I am brave. I ran with the thing that runs beside us. Gum-trees rustled rapturous applause. A huddle of fledglings in a crown cried out commingled, pleading. A raindrop hit my lips and triggered a chant. *Nobody can kill, Huckle-berry-Finn, Nobody can kill, Huckle-berry Finn.* My nape prickled. My soles drummed.

I whipped around in fright at a leaf skittering. A heavy wooden gate swung into a wall with a noise like a gunshot. A clang of flailing wind-chimes throttled itself. I ran from the thing that runs behind us.

I came to her street with soles burning.

Hers was the only house with a single light on. The blind in the window was only half shut, and in the cracks, molten orange glowed. On the stake in the yard the ice-cream lid quivered. I hurried past telling myself it was only to see the place from a different angle.

Pacing by the empty block, I glanced, again and again, at the window.

Fingers sweat around the stone. Claw-fingers stiffened.

The stone was not enough – nowhere near enough. The stone was too much.

The stone was too much and I was too afraid to go any closer and throw it – to do what I'd come for.

An empty can of Sunkist clattered in the gutter by the vacant block.

No streetlight cast in the block. No moonlight cast in the block. Collared on brambles, a white plastic-bag flapped like a white, ghostly flag.

Standing at the kerb, I peered, for what must've been a while, at the lot's blindfold-black middle, right into its heart. I suppose I became transfixed. I convinced myself that I saw something it wasn't possible to have seen. I saw the dog. I saw him in the block's quintessence – front paw cocked, looking right back at me, as if he was wondering what I was doing here, and why he too, was here. From my scalp, down my neck and spine, all the way into my toenails, I tingled. I whispered his name. I said it aloud but he'd forgotten his own name. Hoping to startle him into visibility I underarmed the stone, lobbed it in a gentle arc, near to the spot. The stone suspended, like something playfully thrown, one hand to another on the moon.

The stone came back to earth.

Nothing moved.

Nothing reappeared.

The wind went to ground.

The lot was spiritless, emptier than it had ever been.

In another street somewhere, a dog was barking. Closer to the highway another dog reacted. A third, more distant, deeper bark joined in. Now two others pitched in. Dog after dog roused inflamed, perplexed, decrying the outrage. Voices relayed and ricocheted and ran across the night. All at once altogether they were in fullest cry.

All at once, altogether, they were silent.

Something passed.

The wind swung around and the night's animal-spirit voice redoubled. I set foot on the block, and ventured in all the way and searched in nearsighted circles straining my eyes, until I was bamboozled and frightened and fled.

I came alongside the park, where gumtrees swayed, and mourned.

Jeremy

The summer before high school I spent with a frothy haired, flush-cheeked kid called Jeremy Lyon.

I remember a Confirmation card on his bedside table – a lion atop a mountain, emblazoned by a bloody African sun.

To our brave, loyal Jeremy, take all before you that's yours.

Fear not the jackals.

In the ocean his curls matted a deep piss-yellow. Giddy with ocean oxygen, contorting with laughter at anything and anyone: a hairy Greek fleeing the waves with tennis-ball testicles bobbing in Speedos and gold chains glittering; a scrawny kid shivering transfixed by nothing; a man in sudden middle-age examining his very own newfound breasts.

The words he managed after seeing me dumped by an ocean wave the first time still trumpet in my ears, when the ocean makes a fool of me.

The Evil Dog's been ambushed!

Throwing his head back, swallowing sun.

He had to swallow his mother's suicide, a couple of summers down the track.

Our friendship had come adrift only a couple of months before, after he changed schools.

My mother told me the strange news. I remember it was a school night. I remember it was raining. And the disappointed look she gave me when I delayed picking up the phone, as if what had happened was an inconvenient interruption.

I remember dialling in slow-motion, pausing ten, fifteen seconds before dialling the last digit. Before connection there was a strange unexplained silence, like the house itself had died. The first ring sounded like a scream.

Each unanswered ring edged me closer to an excuse to put down the phone. Rain drummed the roof. Through the kitchen window a cat stranded in the deluge slunk down the other side of the dripping fence.

A remote, flattened voice: Jeremy's.

I remember stilted questions. 'Does anyone – does anyone know why she did it?'

'Not fully.'

'Not even – not even your dad?'

'Not fully.'

Pause.

On the kitchen window a fly left over from summer took confused, jerky, diagonal steps. On the other side rain squiggled and ran down the glass in miniature tributaries.

'Is it – is it raining really hard up there?'

'It was before.'

In the background his sister said something, to their dad, maybe. Jeremy turned from the phone, softly said something.

Somebody might've been crying.

When he came back to the phone, I could hear his breathing. I couldn't think what to say next. My head was hollow. My footing had shifted, and staring where two sheets of wallpaper overlapped, I said, 'Maybe I'll come around, some day. Maybe I'll ride my bike up there.'

His reply was drowned in hardened rain. There are moments we should ask someone to repeat something – we do it easily enough, when talk is inconsequential. There are moments we should stay put and listen, no matter how long it takes.

'You sound really far away.'

'Probably just the rain,' Jeremy said.

'I really liked her ... she was ... ace, your mum.'

His answer was just a raw half-sound somewhere in his throat – an unclassifiable, muted, gutted sound. I remember staring down at the brass strip where the slatted sliding door to the lounge-room ran, unsure he was still there. I remember counting breaths.

I remember doing something small to Judy Lyon one night, over her specialty desert: cheesecake embedded with kiwi. The memory of my childish ruse can still make me wince.

She'd asked me did my Irish father have an Irish temper. I'd shaken my head coyly, a kind of spontaneously insincere shyness.

She chuckled with a trace of gentle, purely sociable mischief. With her dessert fork she raised cheesecake to her lips, and said she wouldn't mind betting he had a devil of a temper. '*All* Irishmen have short fuses.'

I gave a curt shake of the head – raising the stakes.

Judy Lyon said, 'I'll bet it's *red* hot, is it?'

Feigning more discomfort – too late to pull out now – I kept my eyes lowered.

Her husband said to her, 'I think our guest has answered that question.'

She measured a response, measuring spoonful of cheesecake. 'I was only asking a question, Ron.'

'Yes, but you didn't seem to like the answer.'

For some reason she was humiliated, blushing crimson. I felt the prick of shame – as if I'd kicked a softly inquisitive, harmlessly prickly creature.

She said without looking at him, 'I'll just sit here contributing nothing then.'

'Nobody's asking any such thing,' Ron Lyon answered, 'nobody's persecuting anybody.'

She put her spoon down, gave him a direct, meaningful look. Jeremy blushed, glancing from his mum to his sister. His sister glanced at her mum, then her dad, back to Jeremy. Somehow nobody looked at me.

Judy Lyon had a rich, gravelly voice, with the scrupulous enunciation of a primary-school teacher. 'When you boys fall in love, you'll be twice as handsome overnight.' And, 'Don't believe it when they tell you nothing lasts, boys. Ronald and I are sixteen years strong. All the other bozos stood me up or left me for dead, but the night I met Ronald they faded to dust.'

Reserved and rangy, each year Ron Lyon ran The Big M Melbourne Marathon – running with aloof resolve, as if he'd suffered an acute humiliation when he was younger and would always be squaring the ledger. Whenever our dads were thrown together for a few minutes, mine assumed a serious expression and

Jeremy's stood in a way he must have thought looked loose.

I remember Ron Lyon driving us to the ocean in his Army-green Commodore Executive. On the undulating entrance road Jeremy and I were on the edge of the seat, straining seatbelts, glimpsing waves carrying the ocean's breadth, all its might, rumbling all the way from another world. Over snowy avalanche waves drifted a mist of effervescent ocean essence. Between the flags, bathers milled. Further out, in a rarefied realm, surfers and seabirds glided. Jeremy would say, 'I could live without anything but the ocean.'

His father, in ritual reflex: 'What about oxygen?'

On the way home dusk whipped through the car, muffling and amplifying the radio songs of that summer: Love Is a Battlefield and Come Said the Boy, and a song that followed Jeremy and I that summer.

Wake-up-tooo-a-brand —newww-day

Find-your-dreams-haveWASHedawaay

I remember Judy Lyon pulling over to the roadside, turning her face to her window, bottom lip trembling with emotion.

Jeremy beside her, asking, 'Mum … what's the matter? Did somebody do something to you?'

I remember a motorbike passing rocking the car.

Jeremy saying, 'You know I'll keep it between you and me, Mum.'

In the silence the dashboard clock's tick sounded like a bomb ticking down.

She told him not to worry, that the person making her life hell would soon go away.

She told him he would grow up to be a great painter, and told me I would win the Pulitzer Prize.

'Whatever's wrong Mum … whatever it is . . . we can fix it.' Jeremy smoothing her frizzy hair, stroking with his palm.

And her turning to him fighting tears. '*Jeremy Ronald Lyon.*' Bunching a fistful of his curls. 'Somewhere there's a *lucky* girl.'

Summer holidays in Australia had longevity. Days entwined, enshrined in sun. Jeremy and I roamed Mount Martha's unpaved roads breathing shrub-scented dust, trespassing holiday-home gardens, bombing strangers' pools.

One afternoon we were detained and entertained, and had our imaginations stoked, by two women who could only have been lovers.

We were just about to take a running leap into a favourite pool when a woman appeared on a patio, hailing us like long-lost sons. She wore a glossy parakeet-green headscarf and gypsy earrings.

'If she's half as nuts as she looks,' said Jeremy, 'we're in for a tragic end to our sad little lives, Dog.'

As we came closer, she said, 'I've been expecting you or someone very like you – my stars foretold this.' She sounded European – Dutch, maybe German; or Belgian or Czech, or Scandinavian.

We found ourselves in a cavernous kitchen, where there were a lot of pans and pots and utensils hanging from hooks, and herbs strung up. On a benchtop was an open bottle of Brown Brothers white wine and some crackers and cheese.

She pointed us down a hall to something she called a sitting-room, promising us something cold to drink.

In the hall Jeremy said under his breath, 'La di-da, Dog, we're off to the sitting-room. Prepare to sit and rotate.'

'Maybe we're about to become experiments. I read about these kids that got lured by a cult and got injected and brainwashed and turned into slaves.'

'Jesus, Dog, calm down.'

In the sitting room a soft-bosomed younger woman in a burgundy summer dress stroked a grey-blue cat on a bamboo-frame couch with giant, soft white cushions. They might've been lounging on a cloud. She gave us an unhurried, unsurprised smile, took a last, deep, unremorseful drag on a cigarette. As she leant to stub it in the ashtray on a coffee-table, we saw the shadow of her cleavage – the cat unfurled and shot from the room as if our coming had soured things. The woman said hello, asked who we might be and what we were doing here. Jeremy said we were secret agents.

'What sort of a secret agent doesn't keep it secret?'

'A crappy one.' He asked if she lived here.

She shook her head, looked at him.

'We've ruined your peace and quiet haven't we?'

'Nope,' she said, 'wasn't doing much . . . sitting here patting a cat and thinking.'

'What about?'

She looked away. On the table in front of her a glass of wine caught the sun. 'Well . . . if you must know, I was thinking about freedom.'

Jeremy turned and looked at a painting on the wall. Something about it struck him at once.

'What about freedom?'

'How it's nice to be free from living in a box.'

'What kind of box?'

'A box somebody tried to fit me into – make that squash.'

Jeremy stared at the painting. There and then the pitch of his voice dropped a register forever. 'Who painted this?'

The first woman reappeared carrying a chilled Mello Yellow can and two glasses in one hand, and a plate of strawberries in the other. She asked Jeremy if he liked what he was seeing.

'I'm jealous.'

'Of?'

'Whoever painted it.'

The woman looked at each other. The one on the couch asked if he painted. He nodded just as if she'd asked if he played Monopoly. But Jeremy painted like nobody in our class. (Once, we'd all been asked to paint a sunset. He painted a nude man and woman running into the sea, hand-in-hand. When Jodie Grundy asked why the water was purple, he said it wasn't, but they'd remember it that way.)

Now he said, 'Without the falcon it would suffer. The falcon does something for the cloud and the cloud does something for the chimney-smoke.'

The women shared another, surprised sort of a look. The one on the couch said they'd love to see one of his paintings, some day – maybe he'd even find his first buyer in this very room.

Goosebumps spread along his triceps. The hair on his forearms stood. He blinked and turned, and stared directly at the shape of her breasts.

The woman in the headscarf let the drinks de-fizz. 'If you paint half as well as you leap into strange people's pools ... I'm sure your technique is bold.'

'Raw,' said the friend.

'With a penchant for full moons.'

Jeremy took a glass, blushing. 'Didn't like to see all that expensive chlorine going to waste.'

The first woman said, 'We only ever swim at night.'

The other gave her a smile I'd never seen one woman give another.

Wheeling our bikes away in the heat, Jeremy ventured, 'Just think Dog ... they're in there right now ravaging each other's lesbian juices on those Laura Ashley cushions.'

'They haven't had time to undress.'

'Wouldn't stop those two nymphomaniacs.'

'They can't help it. They're born that way. They had a show about it on *60 Minutes*.'

'Don't think those two *wanna* help it, Dog. They're busy with their sitting-room orgies.'

We started downhill bumping along the ripples on the gritty, sandy road.

'Feel the vibrations, Dog.'

I'd been lumped with his sister's pink Malvern Star again. Anita Lyon was fifteen but her bike, replete with big yellow daisy-bell and yellow basket, was the same she'd ridden at twelve. Jeremy called it The Dorothy Contraption. Rarely did he laugh with quite the same jubilance as when its pedals gave way with a loud, brittle crunch. On his own bike for some reason Jeremy hardly ever stood out of his seat. If we wanted to go faster he just peddled harder and looked a bit too eager. Playing football, he looked as if he was running on the spot. In cricket he batted like a drunken woodchopper, bowled like he was lobbing grenades, and stood under any catch stifling doomed laughter. The pool was all his. Jeremy's supple buoyant body carved the water leaving outboard churn. In the heats, he'd finish body-lengths in front, watching the scrap for second with his goggles off. Interschool medallions and sashes in gold and royal blue and ribbons of crimson swathed his bedroom wall, but he cared little for them. A poster of Kim Wilde in faded Levis had a more intimate place.

We hauled uphill, to the tennis-courts.

On the bottom court, we lay on our backs, talking in prematurely nostalgic tones about the girls of grade six. Primary school was over but somehow we hadn't shaken its spirit. Jeremy's crush was green-eyed Melissa Nicholson. Occasionally – just often enough to keep him at her altar – she regarded Jeremy with something more promising than amusement. On school athletics day she and stocky Sally Sullivan took turns eclipsing each other and pretending not to notice each other. Sally muscled across the grass in strapping bursts. The object of Jeremy's desire was frictionless, feline, pigtails bobbing like frayed rope, eyes for the string. My crush on her best friend Paula Mason was not exactly imaginative. Paula was so pretty it was hard to look. Not that Jeremy and I lacked imagination. In our phantasmagoria of fantasies, the zenith – thanks to a *Penthouse* Jeremy shoplifted – was a steamy Roman bath. A woman with a river of chestnut hair, and an exotic forest between her legs, was perched on the spa's edge, head thrown back. A tanned, rippling man bowed, worshipping – face nestled in a tender, myste-rious place. *And the wind whispered within her*. Never had we seen such enchanted perfection. Never had we read such exalted excellence.

The baking asphalt pressed heat into our bodies.

Behind our eyes the sun made gauzy cellophane hues swirl and overlap.

On court above, a man and woman found rhythm. Their camaraderie, buoying each other.

'Hey Dog what's the dirtiest thing you've seen your parents do?' Jeremy ventured, "if I tell you something absolutely filthy – promise not to tell.'

Behind my eyes cerise morphed to bloodiest red, through garish green. 'Promise.'

'I once saw Mum and Dad hop in the shower together. I heard the entire horny little conversation.' His voice floated away. 'No way would they shower together anymore.'

A small plane's lazybones drone meshed with the drone of someone mowing. In the bay, a speedboat bumped and purred.

A vermilion money-spider ventured into the glade between my forefinger and thumb, lit out for the wrist.

When he spoke again he sounded like he was sleep talking. 'Imagine not having a mum.'

I sat up, finessing the money-spider to the asphalt.

Jeremy said, over a ripple of laughter surfacing, 'It'd be sheer bloody hell living just with your old man.'

'Imagine never being born.'

'I was meant to live.' He rolled to his side, rested one side of his face in his open palm. 'My family was meant for each other. I can feel it, Dog.'

'Imagine one of your parents were never born.'

'Imagine time traveling all the way back to your parent's honeymoon and watching them humping the exact same night your mum got pregnant. Imagine watching your own gory little birth.'

He sat up. Beads of sweat dotted his forehead. Wisps gilded translucent earlobes. 'Imagine opening your front-door on your wedding anniversary and springing your wife and some hairy stranger rooting like horny little rabbits. I'd run and get a shotgun.'

A scorched jumping-jack landed between us.

'Dog if you could come back as anybody, who would it be?'

'Me.'

'Me too. Sometimes I wonder how anyone can bear not being me.'

We rode to the pine forest and made our ritual pact not to speak until we reached the other side.

Twenty-one minutes had elapsed when we emerged in the clearing. In burnt-blue sky a solitary, cotton-wool cloud floated.

I drew up a cat-tail, smelt the milky root, and bound it to my left wrist.

'Mum comes here,' Jeremy said, looking around, 'she keeps asking me to paint it.' A smell of dried out needles carried from the forest-floor, on a breeze. 'She says I can remember her by it when she's gone. I called her a morbid hound from hell.'

A bronzed dragonfly clutched a cat-tail as though savouring a last kiss. In its wings the finest latticework of tiny veins showed. The tail twitched. The cat-tail quivered in reaction. I felt, right there, an abrupt unexplainable conviction Jeremy and I would soon be strangers. I turned away, actually ran through a swathe of cattails, knees lifting high . . .

On the other side of the clearing I wandered, keeping eyes down. Jeremy called something but his words didn't make it. He repeated it, laughing. For some reason at that moment I'd shut my eyes. And I experienced, distinctly and vividly, what might've been a premonition: a mental picture of him crumbling to his knees at the edge of a lake, weeping. The image did not dissolve after a second or two. It was like it was scorching itself to my conscious mind.

'Dog!' He came stepping through the cat-tails, giddy. 'Dog you are one chronically morbid beast.'

I made some joke, shut my eyes again – the picture had faded, but its contour was branded.

'That's what I like about you, Dog, you're a real live basket-case. A puzzling freak.'

I nodded distractedly, egging him on.

'You're a sad old beast.'

In the grass, a silvery clip on a blue pen-lid reflected the sun.

'You're a moody blue. A morbid hound in a world of pain and sorrow.'

We finished the day visiting the same ill-fated address we often did. Jeremy said, as if he only ever came here to appease me, 'The day just isn't complete for you without a visit to the gruesome shit-pile, is it Dog?' But Jeremy was as intrigued as I was by the forlorn, abandoned air of that forsaken place.

Two years ago, it had been all over the news. Judy Lyon even drove the long way out to the esplanade to avoid its sight. 'That bloodcurdling place will crumble like a stale biscuit before anyone calls it home again. Nobody in their right mind can feel comfortable in a house where a maniac harpooned her poor wretch of a philandering husband through the heart while he dreamt of greener pastures. I mean what a price to charge somebody for their vanity. What a cursed place.'

We stood at the scrappy driveway's mouth. The overrun yard was scattered with knobbly, pock-marked rocks. Dandelions nodded, in evening breeze.

Somewhere an all-seeing bird warned us away. *No NO . . . Don't Go! No . . . NO.* We started down the gravel. A fat feral cat slunk n under the house, as we took the shaky wooden steps to the wraparound porch.

On the other side of a streaky bay window, a huntsman spider was wrapped around a doorknob.

Ceiling fan wings accrued dust, dumbly indifferent.

On the edge of a curtain, a tiny loose cotton thread made what must've been the slightest movement physically possible.

Every time we came here I felt more sympathy for the woman than for her slain husband. Jeremy had admitted the same feeling. The man's pain, we reasoned, was over and done.

Riding away I fired the usual questions. Why did she do it? Because he was leaving her for another woman, Jeremy said. Why didn't she just have an affair, too? She wanted revenge, Jeremy said. But didn't she know she'd get caught? She wasn't thinking clearly, he said. She was only feeling.

Riding at his side I turned the words over ... affair ... revenge ... revenge ... affair ...

Sun filtering through the bushes dappled and flashed on his hair. From the ram's-curl at his temple, sweat trickled, cheek to jaw. I stood and coasted: the pedals ruptured. He cackled throwing his head back

and hunched again, gripping the handlebars, drawing
away; trusting the days ahead.

Basic Introduction to Korean Characters

Two Saturday nights that summer. One I spent in their home playing board-games and singing Beatles songs, sipping a beer, listening to a storm.

The other I saw their home decimated and dishonoured.

South Korea, 2002.

I lived in a cabin, on the grounds of a disused primary-school.

Retired classrooms breathed chalky deep silence.

A gravel-grit half-acre made a weekend football-pitch for locals.

A retired fishing vessel hosted children playing pirates, brandishing sticks for cutlasses and holding each other prisoner. And occasionally teenagers, holding each other close under the moon.

Somehow the place had been spared bulldozing when a new school had gone up, down the road.

Somehow the cabin in a far corner became housing for the local English teacher.

Somehow I'd become that teacher. Morning and early afternoon I taught high-school. Evenings in a small city a half hour drive north, I tutored a trusty reliably restless handful of children, before finishing with businessmen.

A handsome couple and two teenage boys lived in the only other cabin on the grounds. Arriving home in the dark, my first few nights, I'd find offerings at my cabin door: fresh-picked spinach with blackish sheen; thumping sweet potato; glossy chillies; bulging bottles of mountain-water.

The first time I made it over to their place I found the sliding-door wide open to genial midday sun. Her hair was coiled like a beehive under a white towel, and her willowy frame cocooned in a terry-towel dress-ing-gown. Her hips had the abrupt jut and generous shape I hadn't yet recognized as a physical feature of a lot of women here.

I'd come with a makeshift offering of my own, the only two CDs I hadn't given away on leaving Sydney: Jeff Buckley's *Grace* and Hendrix's *Bold as Love*.

Opening them in shampoo-scented sunlight she looked intrigued, quietly amused.

Choosing *Grace,* she went to a portable CD player nestled on a small, neat, blonde bookshelf. 'You teaching me,' she said, smiling to herself, putting the disk in, 'you teacher, me child.' There was a surety about her, as if she'd preconceived the scene. I found myself cross-legged on the floor, tacking on words to a modest English lexicon she was immediately, openly, curiously keen to cultivate.

She made clove tea. She poured almonds into a bowl.

'More learn,' she said, more than once. 'You me teach.'

With a class two hours from now and no lesson ready, I was conscious of time.

'Me many friend,' she said, before I left, that first day, as if the point was crucial in some way, 'every year, many friends.'

I wondered which word to teach. Personable was pallid and sociable not much better, and soulful a bit blurry. She learned 'gregarious', wrote it down, said it aloud a few times, as I poured her more tea.

She had these dark, intensely astute, overtly sensual eyes. 'Now we also are friends.' The tone was apprehensive, assured and discreet, all in the same breath. We touched teacups. She proposed, in the modulated, measured way I would come to know, that we do this each day at this same hour. I felt myself nodding away; as if more teaching was just the thing for a part of the day I'd set aside to recover and prepare.

Her life had a painful humiliating side – a side unseen.

There were signs.

Later, there was evidence. I saw what I wanted to see.

At first, I didn't understand why she was so keen to improve at English. My citified thinking posited possible motives: she was setting an example to her sons, or hoping to emigrate, or fallen for an English-speaking customer in one of the teahouses she worked. That she liked learning for the hell of it might've hardly ever crossed my mind.

We had such an easy rapport. And we found an easy, natural rhythm. Five or six new words a day, with mercifully limited forays into grammar. Some mornings we just chatted in our way, using whatever words we'd accrued – a kind of vocally assisted charades, all exaggerated expressions and gesticulations, often blighted by my stabs at Korean, and always peppered with laughter. I'd never met anyone so quick to laughter.

And I hadn't met many who got me laughing so often.

She was unusually candid. Without prompting, she'd confide. And sometimes I had the feeling she was waiting for me to confide more; to delve deeper into whatever dance it was we were dancing.

With the cicadas shrieking outside one broiling morning she told me she'd never expected to be a mother. 'When I am very young I am…' In her Korean-English dictionary she found *wayward* and *spirited* and *bold.*

Entering the words in her notebook, with the faintest, furtive smile, she asked if I was bold and spirited.

I couldn't honestly say I'd led a bold life. Spirited, yes. But not bold. The admission felt strange. Somehow it felt like telling her I was half-hearted and wanting in an indefinable, probably crucial way.

She said her younger son worried her. He was going through the motions in his final high-school year, in danger of going nowhere. 'If my sons find not happiness – I find not happiness.'

'Understand.' *Ai dah*. Understand.

At the kitchen window, in the persimmon tree, a tiny bird chatted to itself in the most minor key.

She looked at the floor. 'Sometimes difficult life. Helping friends we must.'

We touched teacups.

The bird chirruped. The sky was iris-blue.

When she first saw me, she said, she saw someone who worries too much. 'Every day you are too much thinking, too much worry.'

She learnt *intuition*. I learnt *pontelyo*. And as I left that morning she wrote something in her spiral notepad, tore out the page.

Genchanio.

Don't be afraid.

She began sending one or the other son to my door, Saturdays, inviting me over to lunch.

Sitting on the floor in their easy company beat meals cooked and eaten in self-absorption.

The food was plentiful and straight from the earth: steaming sweet-potato; a smoky, deliciously salty local fish with a pearly spine; clear seaweed soup; sumptuous strawberries. And milk. Chilled milk, in a granite jug, passed around like a peace pipe.

One Sunday morning she passed, on her way to her van, as I worked in the sun outside my cabin.

One of her eyes was blackened. I thought it was some kind of make-up mishap, running late.

She told me she'd had an accident late last night driving her employer's delivery van. She professed embarrassment about the damage to the van. 'Very expensive my fault,' she said, with a convincing laugh.

I heard what I wanted to hear.

How to introduce the fisherman?

The fisherman had shoulders hard as bollards and a neat pink scar over one eyebrow. I had the feeling he was something of an outsider, wherever he was. When she or one of the boys tried a little English, he looked bewildered, a tad slighted. The little he said in his own language sounded shy, purely functional.

In bluntly unadmiring looks the second son directed at him, I saw nothing serious, just a little teenage mutiny.

Seventeen-year-old Ki Won had his mother's cheek-bones. She'd once told me that since he was tiny, he'd talked and dreamt of riding a motorbike the length of Korea.

Ki had a tight circle of friends, of which he appeared to be something of an axis.

Alone, tending to stoop, eyes often fixed on the ground, he seemed to be injured in some unseen way

– recovering from or circling around the solution to something.

His posse knocked on my bungalow door one clammy Sunday afternoon, asking if I wanted to go with them to the mountain. I had an inkling they'd been put up to it, out of hospitality, but if any resented it, they had the grace not to show it. The tallest had a rangy lope, to match a mellow grin. A skinnier rubbery-faced comically animated character with unusually high pitch kept everyone laughing with a relentless running commentary of which I couldn't understand a word, but somehow couldn't help laughing at. The other kid just looked tough. Ki walked in the middle.

The path to the mountain wound fifteen, maybe twenty minutes.

When we entered the mountain trail the comedian asked, in his most nonchalant tone, what I thought about schoolboys who smoked cigarettes. I told him I strongly disapproved, but the unintentional shrug I gave didn't exactly stiffen the message.

So began a charade – and, uncomfortable to admit, mine. By turns they slipped away from the trail, into the forest, sheepishly reappearing chewing cinna-mon-scented gum. I played along, pretending not to notice.

I kept my eyes peeled for other, more interesting things, hoping as always to sight the resident eagle – a bird either reclusive, passed away or entirely legendary. Up here there was always plenty else to see: squirrels glancing down from munching some kind of nutty treat growing wild; and the miniscule serrated leaf, carpeting parts of the trail by the tonne, fallen from who knew where – I could never find its source-tree, and in a funny way, preferred not to.

Half an hour after starting, we'd reached the steepest part of the trail and halfway mark. Alone, right here, I'd always turn and start down again.

Ki Won said they had something to show me, higher.

For months I'd been postponing higher ground, waiting for a day the decision to come to Korea was proved, by some superficial measure of the superego, Unambiguously Correct – a day I would soar, or so I believed, free of all doubt and human frailty. Now, alas, I had no choice but to surrender the grand plan.

We trudged up a spirally rise of close-packed, strong-smelling earth. There was a clearing, a kind of tableland. At one end, overlooking the steel-blue bay stood a waist-high ring of rocks. It was there, they appeared to be leading me.

At first it struck me as a modest thing. Inside the ring, thistles outnumbered daisies. Inside the ring, sour-smelling weeds outnumbered the daisies. It looked like some sort of ceremonial site, gone to pasture. I pictured a soaring moon, drummers, dancing; a rites-of-passage ritual reverberating in fiery dark.

The truth was less romantic. From inside the ring, for hundreds of years, people had watched for dragon boats, come from Japan, to plunder.

Ki told me Korea had successfully defended herself against Japan more than two-hundred times. Clearly, they were proud of that. I found myself proud of it, too. The tough-looking kid said that sometimes, in Korea, people who drove Japanese cars came out of the supermarket to find their tyres mysteriously deflated. A collective sheepish smile spread from each to the next, as if it was unfortunate, but not something that could really be stopped.

The rough-hewn rocks were unexpectedly warm to touch. The smell was dusty with hints of salt and lime.

Standing inside I imagined myself on watch, and wondered what the punishment for dozing on the job had been: sincere self-reproach might not have cut it here in 1417. Even now, there was something exacting in the life here, something hardnosed. I considered asking them if they felt this – that Korea could be unforgiving. And I decided, as usual, the question could wait. Shelving curiosity to avoid offending anyone at any cost was a longstanding deficiency of mine. And if it was true that people appreciated tact – nobody likes having their culture nit-picked by a foreigner – it was also true I rarely came away from any exchange, or even any extended encounter much the wiser.

We all took turns standing on the ancient ring of rocks. In good spirits the boys posed and ribbed.

Ten, fifteen minutes later, having re-entered the trail and resumed the climb, we came to rest on a ruffled ledge, sipping water bottled at the trail. A gate in the clouds opened and the sun stepped out. The bay twin-kled east to west, as if a giant hand were passing over, disseminating glitter.

Ki rested a hand on my shoulder, pointed at the dwarfed grounds of the school. 'Number One glamour address.'

We slapped high-five.

I found myself focusing on the just-discernible bungalow, as if long-distance examination would reveal its true nature: hidey-hole to someone on the run from life, or home to someone brave enough to turn his life upside down? At least I was on a mission to become something more, this time.

So why did I feel, even in a moment like this, that my life was in Sydney wondering where I'd gotten; or somewhere else entirely, waiting for me to come meet it?

I'd make these clichéd lists of places I sensed I'd be better suited: Dublin, Madrid, Tokyo.

Ki's elder brother Jung Won saw one such list accruing dust on top of my little fridge, one afternoon, and asked, in his disarmingly artless way, what it meant.

'Probably nothing … my lists come to nothing … signify nothing. They're ruses, illusions, diversions.'

He responded the way he always did if ever I lapsed into English he had no hope of understanding – with a flourish of Korean I had no hope of understanding and a boyish smile. Jung spoke and moved as if he hadn't a combative bone in his body. It often seemed to me there was strength in that, alone.

He worked ten days at a time in a city two hours west, and then came home for a week. Whenever he was home, he and I would fill backpacks with plastic bottles and take the curling trail to the foot of the mountain, where the clearest, coldest water flowed for anybody who cared to bottle it.

On our walk one afternoon I asked him to describe a typical day in the restaurant. In his Korean-English dictionary he found anarchic (*mujongbu*), slavedriver (*chimulhul*) and stimulating (*chaguk*). He asked me to describe teaching Korean teenagers and I showed him *imsigong* (ad-libbing), *musikhan* (unqualified) and *mu jil so* (chaos).

On the way back I asked him something I don't think I'd ever asked another person – probably because I preferred not to have to answer it, in turn. I asked did he have a single overriding ambition, something he wanted more than anything else in the world. He answered without hesitation: he wanted a family, wanted to be a father, a provider, to give everything, all his effort and energy, all his love, so that the people he loved would be happier. 'This is true happiness,' he said, as if it was plain as day and happily irrefutable.

On the other side of the bridge the question rebounded. I was older than him by ten years but you wouldn't have known it – I ducked and weaved and deviated and backtracked until a merciful palm landed on my shoulder. 'Okay, okay Mr Patrick.' He smiled without a trace of meanness or mockery, tugged a cat-tail from the roadside, held it like a microphone and murdered a Korean pop-song the rest of the way home.

Soon after, deep in a Saturday night, their lives capsized. Only one of them was at home.

Smashing glass noises woke me in the dark. Every muscle was on high-alert, like I'd been forewarned in a dream. Conversely, confusingly, not a muscle moved. Another smash – closer. In perverse paralysis, recalling my recent short fuse in class, I pictured a posse of older brothers come to teach the foreigner humility. I sprang and yanked on cut-off cords and, keeping low, moved closer to the sliding front door.

Suddenly I was certain someone was outside, behind the door, just to the side. The steel claw on the door, as usual, was unlocked. Moonlight glazed the mock-cedar linoleum. My toes and the balls of my feet dug in disinclined to take another step – for a farcical moment I regretted not having started karate lessons at thirteen, one Tuesday night, with my best friend, Adam Combes, in the shire hall: a calamitous decision taken lightly.

My sense that someone was patiently waiting outside firmed. I straightened up.

Ear to door I listened.

I flung open the sliding door with a ludicrous leap – primed to hit the ground running or swinging. Instead I was disarmed by the sky. Even for here, it was truly wild – a miracle made by something beyond words, names, forms. Swarming incandescent stars scattered to every plot and pocket. Stars pressed down right in your face. They were enough to hold you there, keep you craning, dizzy with purest wonder and dumbstruck awe.

I blinked. Whiffs of smoke carried.

And a plaintive voice pleading, crying. It seemed to be coming from the other cabin. I turned, groped along my own cabin's flank.

Not ten feet from their door, a dying bonfire pulsed without sound. For a terrifically stupid moment I assumed it was ritualistic – something marking summer's passing; something nobody had mentioned. For a few steps I was even disappointed at being excluded. Closer, the fire emitted something desolate.

Closer again I saw just how unceremonious.

The fisherman hunched at the scrappy fire's smouldering fringe. Pleading into his phone, beseeching, intoxicated by a fiery spirit, his balance wavered, as if trying to keep his footing in a squall.

I came to a stop, profoundly dumb, at his side.

In one hand he gripped the phone: in the other a long-handled spade.

A prostrate clothes rack on the fire discharged a sour stench of plastic melting. He was burning her clothes: every stitch. Underwear shrivelled, as if in shame. A canary-yellow silk scarf so far unharmed all at once shrivelled.

A pink, furry slipper smoked at the very edge.

Nobody was in the bungalow.

Nobody, it struck me, had been there all day.

The fisherman tossed the phone on the flames. If I stayed another moment, something urgent told me, I'd be spliced – he roared as if he'd been speared in the heart and turned, swinging the spade high, like a harpoon, rupturing the sliding door with a devastating crash that shook the very stars.

Running for the main gate, passing her parked van I saw the windows smashed, glass ringing the van like frost shaken off a tree. The police-station was less than ten minutes if I kept running hard.

The balls of my feet slapped the pavement by the road. A streaky shooting star dived behind the mountain – I envisaged, in a moment of madness, hiking later on tonight, staying up for sunrise. Then I'd have a story. I heard myself appraising the situation in this way; grading its raw materials. Iyagi. Story. Tal yeon byeon. Deserter. A police van passed, pulsing mute, aimed for the grounds. Somebody had beat me there. Somebody must've heard, even seen. Kow jong. Violence. Fury. Danger.

After the station I took the long way home, through the ricefields. In the dark they smelled different, more of crop water, than grain. Fireflies oscillated. Standover pylons loomed iron-fisted. Only one thing I knew of incited that sort of wretched rage in a man: another man. Almost every adult knew the feeling of having been betrayed. Whether she'd betrayed him was unclear and beside the point.

The truth was I could've been the other man, if I'd been wayward and spirited and treacherous enough. Memory of the night was still fresh ... She'd parked the van, with only the two of us, by the gates, only a little deeper into the grounds, so that we were facing the poplars. The cooling engine ticked. The moon cast light on the bonnet. An hour ago I'd watched her leading a dance troupe on an open air stage.

She rested a hand, lightly, on my thigh, just above the knee.

Her hair was let down and the scent of it charged the air.

I took her hand, lifted it, returning it like a gift neither of us could afford. 'Unwise.'

'Unwise?' Showing a wry, unselfconscious smile, she'd stared through the windscreen. Unwise. *Orisokun chon anin.*

Now, as I walked, that moment felt more significant.

Another piece of the puzzle – a Sunday she'd driven us to another town to meet a friend of hers, a sculptor and bowl-maker. Their conversation, sitting on the floor in his studio, had been subdued, intense, as if they were afraid of someone. I'd left them and gone walking. On returning, they were still sitting facing, only closer, and more emotional. On the drive home, I'd never even asked her a single question. Without her, I'd have fallen flat on my face here – endured at best. *Kamsa.* Gratitude. No matter who she loved or stopped loving, whatever her weaknesses, she wasn't to blame for *that*, tonight.

A firefly parked in my line at eye-level, waited, pulled ahead. Each time I came close again it repeated the move.

Another, more ordinary exchange resurfaced. She'd once offered the thought, as she poured us tea, that our having met was providence. I'd nodded amiably, more or less leaving the impression I agreed. *So io ui.* Mutual.

Now I wondered what was Korean for misleading, or dupe, or wilfully blind, or embarrassingly naive. A crane stirred in the dark labouring for lift off, breasted the crops with noisy flapping, sweeping away to the other side of the fields. Past the fields, the kids from my classes slept. I felt this rush of affection for every face. Still, in the next step, I couldn't help shake the feeling I'd contributed to the night's violence.

Another shooting star went down. And then another.

Minutes later I stood a stone's throw from the demolished cabin, an onlooker again.

From the back of a squad car the fisherman watched a boyish officer stamping a mulish last flame, singeing a sole, hopping about cussing. An elder officer took a last look in the dwelling, turned, flicked the end of a cigarette at the deadened fire, saw it fall short, ground it with his black boot, rotating from the ankle like he was doing the twist.

Then they were gone and I was standing at the entrance.

Broken glass was everywhere, shards, splinters, mean little glimmering bits. The bookcase lay face down. The TV was obliterated. The new, shared laptop was splayed, trapped under the weight of the overturned desk. Fractured family portraits were stomped, all in splintery schism. At my feet, lay the wooden orthopaedic footboard I used, habitually, whenever I stepped in. I crouched, picked it up. Broken glass slid off, tinkling, like small change.

It hit me, for the first time, how tight it was for two adults and two adolescents. Not once, had I heard any of them complain.

What right did I have to be standing here?

And why the fuck hadn't I stopped him?

In bed I stared at the ceiling, saw a day she and I and the fisherman walked altogether to the mountain. We'd taken photos of each other, self-consciously. Saw him standing tall with his broad back to the crenelated pine, smiling with mock puffed-up pride – like a kid delighting in growing.

Sunday night. The oblong light in my cabin ceiling was expiring, flickering, as if last night had frazzled its nerves. In the silence that fell over the grounds, around this hour, I stood doing the washing up, plotting the working week. The key was to recycle lessons from school to school, preparing two or three a day instead of five. (Six months it had taken me to figure that one.)

Someone rapped the door.

Arms-length, suds to the wrists, I paused before opening.

'*Patrick.*' It was Ki Won. '*My house*?!' Two moths followed him in – one pursuing the other in high-speed chase.

Later that night, Ki would tell me he'd been away for three days on a school camp. But just at that moment, standing with him under the stammering strobe light, I still had no idea where he his mother had been since Friday. I knew that his brother was away working. And I knew what I'd stumbled on in the dark. But I'd spent all Sunday tutoring college kids in the city and had no more information.

Immediately I let him know the damage had been his father's doing. He shook his head and made a doubting sound as if for some reason that couldn't be true. The jittering light was complicating his confusion.

He ran hands over cropped hair, asked me to describe exactly who and what I'd seen.

I acted it out, starting from the moment I'd woken. When I came to the part about the fisherman, his confusion dissipated.

The fisherman, he explained, wasn't his real father.

'My father…' Wrestling with the English he looked at the floor, gripping the air in front of his face. 'Father –' He took his wallet from his jacket pocket, found a small, black and white photograph softened at the corners.

The man in the photograph had high cheekbones, solemn eyes, and an incommunicable sadness.

From on top of the mini-fridge Ki picked up my Korean-English dictionary. He rifled through.

He blushed. The man was *institutionalised, disturbed, unfit mentally.*

Michin.

I'd heard the word thrown around, the way kids do.

I nodded, told him I understood.

With an uneasy smile and nod, he returned the photograph to the wallet.

'Understand,' I repeated, hand tapping heart.

We were silent for some time. The night floated in. I found myself thinking of a photograph turned up in an old wallet only that morning. She too, had once been tagged with a humbling label – one that had nothing to do with her essence. I'd found the photograph stowed away in a bag, with other buried things – things I had no right lumping her in with. I hadn't known she'd come with me again. But I knew only too well that there was nowhere I went or could ever go without the memory of her love. I'd never let go as you were meant to – never even tried. I'd never sought 'closure' because I didn't want 'closure.' I still loved her there didn't seem anything I could do – or even anything she could to – to stop me from loving her.

Seeing her face in the photograph, something unexplainable filled me, as if I was being reminded I was more . . . . Her eyes were unlike anyone's. Her company and replenishing love were unlike anything I'd experienced since. She still had me in her palm, if only she knew. She was recovered, living in another country and probably every bit as vital and brilliant as I'd always known she'd be. Her letters had let me see and feel as much. I couldn't stop loving her, but didn't have the courage to go and find her, or even write and tell her. I was choking on the fear of something terrible happening to her again. And I was just as petrified, if I was honest, of *her* having left *me* behind. Jesus. I was afraid to say her name aloud to myself.

'Patrick you are okay?' The teenager laid a hand on my shoulder.

I nodded, came back, asked where his mother was. Without much conviction, he said she was visiting her mother and sister. I wondered had she known it was coming, if she'd known the fisherman would, for some reason only she knew, detonate.

But if she'd known, why hadn't she gotten a message to her sons?

Ki stared at the cabin floor.

Over his head the moths had forgotten all about the chase. Instead they were lapping the light in opposite directions faster and faster each circuit.

'Your brother?' I said. 'Away? At work?'

Ki nodded, distractedly, stared a hole in the floor.

The moths collided head-on. One crashed into the sink. The other swerved out the door with concussion.

After a time we stepped out, and without speaking went to the shattered home.

After sweeping and bagging up the last of the ruins, we stepped out onto the grass, and watched the stars. Along the road dissecting town, a shuddering semi-trailer discharged a lugubrious honk like a long goodbye.

As I apologised, once again, for not having cleaned up the wreckage, his hand landed on my shoulder and he told me, again, no apology was necessary.

I offered him the spare bed at my place.

He said he'd stay with a family friend, across the fields.

'Well.' I kept eyes on the stars. 'If ever — if your family needs somewhere … I mean your family is . . . I mean if not for your family's friendship — if any of you need my place, I can find somewhere else and you can have mine and . . . I can find another . . . another house and you wouldn't even have to – I mean I wouldn't hesitate to …'

The boy actually smiled, pressing his youthful fist to mine. 'Patrick.' He started away, stepping backwards through dark. 'Patrick, *Genchanio*.'

~

Ka ul. Fall. Autumn swept in. Children raced each other home. Fallen leaves chased each other in circles crackling brown. Morning skies dressed in iris-blue.

On the grounds now, there were these absences: Jung's laughing at a TV show the same time every Sunday night; Ki and his friends crossing the grounds on Friday afternoon. And his mother's friends dropping by to loan a scarf or lend a book or accept something grown in the garden – women who left buoyed. Native levity had moved on.

Kam jong. Sentimental.

And some things were just the same. The communal vegetable-patches drew the same gardeners from the nearest neighbourhood. Tawny-faced figures material-ized digging with claw-tools in gnarled fingers, arms ropey with a lifetime's rigor.

Before, I'd often seen her bring one or another gardener tea and a biscuit, heard her chatting and laughing. Now when those same gardeners stopped to rest they looked at the broken abode not just wistfully, but with something like resignation – as if hers was one more version of a story. I wondered how much they knew.

I wondered how much I knew.

And wondered why, whenever I visited her in their new place, I never could ask about that Saturday night.

The new address hunched in the next town. A low, mottled ceiling sagged. Fissures like forked lightning ran up and down a wall. Their liberty had contracted. Nobody complained. *Geum-yog juujia*. Stoic. *Nag Jeonn*. Faith. Or was it optimism?

Invited to breakfast one Sunday, I leaned in out of the snow bearing gifts, to a startling sight: the fisherman, cross-legged, wrapped in a doona, snug as a kitten, sipping green tea. I couldn't believe my fucking eyes. And he probably couldn't believe his luck when I buried that reaction in an instant mask of blithe geniality. As I reached to meet his extended hand he smiled only a little self-consciously. The scar over his eye looked different now. Once, I'd pictured a fishing mishap – now it looked like someone he'd whacked with a pool-cue had grabbed the nearest glass.

His partner, slicing an apple the size of a crystal ball, wore an illegible smile. I wondered was she only afraid. I wondered how men like him so often managed to regain their place. Could any physical intimacy be worth it? And could a person really be any more secure, with someone volatile?

Another question I might've asked: why people like me didn't do or say more, in a moment just like this? Then again what could I do? Put him in a headlock? Refuse to make small talk? Berate him with the assistance of my pocket-dictionary? Leave? I could leave on principal. I could do that.

I stayed. Of course I stayed. The meal was a bounty, a cure for anything: sizzling cuttlefish, seasoned dried squid, spiced sea-cucumber kimchi, fresh tomato-juice, and local rice so softly ample and aromatic it could've made a meal in itself.

Chopstick pincers click-clacked.

Conversation stammered, made false starts, sparked and stalled again. All the while she kept an eye on her sons – and the fisherman – for signs of discontent. All the while the fisherman glanced from one face to the next, seeking acceptance and it seemed to me, watching for signs of dissent. The brothers, somehow, said nothing directly to each other. Something was wrong between them but whether it was over and above the fisherman's return, I couldn't tell.

After the meal, in frosted sun Ki and Jung and I walked to the baseball nets, a place they'd introduced me to, one I'd taken to stopping at on the way home from work. The nets were open air. After feeding a few coins into a pitching machine, you could swing away stress.

On the walk it became clear that the brothers' difference wasn't something passing. Bruised silence had set hard. I thought of my own brother, strong as three men; saw him setting the pace on another concrete pour under unblinking sun, a T-shirt wrapped around his hot head.

In the nets the brothers experienced a role-reversal. Ki, usually an athletic ace, swung at every ball as if it owed him money, but the bat was like a broken axe in his hands. Jung entered a zone, mysterious and untouchable. Balls sailed to him in slow-motion, sitting up, drawing the bat's sweet spot. When I jacked up the speed on his machine the spell only deepened, quickened. The entire time, his expression was utterly composed and unsurprised.

Afterward, in timid snowfall, Ki went his own way, lighting a cigarette and saying he had someone to meet.

Jung said something scathing and mocking. The retort sounded like a blunt, low blow. In vain I tried to get them to make it up, tried to get them to shake.

Later, sitting with Jung in a coffee-shop window booth, things became less unclear. He told me Ki was becoming wayward – disrespecting his mother, staying out all hours on school nights. One night he'd even come home drunk.

I pictured my brother's turbulence at seventeen. And remembered my own inane bravado, and began to say something about it being a phase, then pictured Ki that Sunday night, as we'd swept the wreckage – what the hell did I know about anything he was feeling?

I asked Jung how drunk his brother had been.

'Patrick … I don't know because I do not ever experience.' He touched the table with the soft underside of his fist. 'Patrick, in Korea if make wrong decisions, this we will…'

'*Hu ho*'. Regret.

'Yes.'

'Understand.' Understand. *Ai dah*.

'My brother now …'

'*Kanyeehada*.' Taking a big risk.

'*Kanyeehada*, yes.'

Lately, in the city, I'd begun noticing Korea did in fact have its share of lost boys: idly angry guys into their twenties hanging around dingy video-games joints. It was impossible to picture Ki becoming one. He was too intrinsically lively, too physical. But nobody was born to lose their way – people *lost* their way. And he didn't have his dad to help straighten the rudder.

I pictured my own dad. Two years had passed since I'd seen his restless blistered hands and smelled his scent: rolled in 2Stroke and cigarettes. Dad and his sprawling, inappropriate, bloody funny jokes.

Jung stared out the window. Sleety, sloppy snow was coming down. On the footpath four tykes in mittens and pom-pom beanies put the brakes on their bikes, craning, catching it on lolling tongues.

Ki reappeared. He walked beside a guy wheeling a muddy lime-green motorbike. The guy said something, eyes ahead. Ki glanced over his shoulder at something, maybe at nothing. As they passed the window, Jung tried to catch his eye. Ki missed him. Then he was walking away again.

I picked up a sugar sachet, flipped it hand to hand, tried to think of something to say.

An old woman stopped to watch a chirruping starling bounce across the footpath to the base of a bare-branch tree, where it had spied a morsel.

'Patrick, you will leave Korea so soon," Jung said, after some time, "but again you will be here.' It sounded half question, half prediction.

One cloudless morning before I left Korea, Mrs. Kim and I chatted in winter sun. She'd come to say hello, come to pull up some greens, fill a few bottles at the foot of the mountain. We were standing on the scrappy gravel between the gates and road, admiring a midday moon transparent as a contact-lens, in boundless powder-blue.

He came snarling past us on a midnight-blue motorbike. No helmet; black kerchief tight to his lips; scarlet bandanna flapping like a flag of flaming youth.

She gaped. 'Ki Won?'

Agitating dust trailed the bike.

'*My* son?' She made an exasperated, deeply motherly, secretly admiring sound.

At the crossroads he slowed, undecided on direction. The motor gurgled. He blazed across the bridge over the river – a river that some weeks turned hard, and others overflowed.

All the way up the mountain with The Americans

The Americans were coming for the weekend. Like me, they were English teachers. Their employer – an old friend of my own employer – was driving them all the way down from Seoul.

The Americans, my employer told me in his keen English, had not yet seen any Korean countryside. His steady eye-contact made it plain who he saw as their weekend guide. I was all set to refuse. Then I pictured myself trading teaching tales, speaking in no-holds barred English, maybe even (gasp!) going for a drink.

He pressed. 'What you now think my idea?'

I filled a Styrofoam cup at his water-cooler, at the window facing the mountain – silhouette didn't do it justice, made it amorphous, even trite. 'When are they arriving?'

'Saturday likely – *much* appreciate. American teachers...' Spreading his fingers, as if holding a ball of energy likely to burn him, handled without care.

'American teachers *much* anticipate meet Australian teacher.'

They came to my cabin on schedule. A bright-eyed stocky guy front and centre sported a T-shirt with a red, white and blue eagle dropping star-spangled bombs:

DESERT STORM!

WE CAME

WE SAW

WE KICKED ASS!

Behind him stood a very tall guy in navy jeans and navy T-shirt, shrewd-eyed in neat spectacles. Even in that first moment he and I seemed to be at odds, in some way.

A third stood off to a side, droopy shouldered with puppy-dog eyes.

'So here he is,' declared Desert Storm. 'Loneliest guy in all Korea.'

'Not true. I have my students, and the stars.'

'Not what we heard,' grinning irresistibly, 'we heard you need some good old native-speaker conversation and a hearty laugh at bad old life!'

I shrugged, a bit thrown, motioning them all in. All left their shoes on, ignoring Korean custom.

Puppy Dog flourished a camera no bigger than a box of matches, snapping the floors and walls and other things in the bungalow. 'It's kinda cool … I mean, at least he's got his own space.' He craned, immortalized the low ceiling.

From the hip-high roof of the mini-fridge Mr Tall picked up the giant leaf, a mellowed mountain memento curling at the edges, like a cupped hand after a long life, replete with raised, encrusted veins. 'How long have you been all the way out here on your own, guy?'

'Six months … Six and a half. Feels like more.'

'That a good or bad thing?' He twirled the leaf from the stem. 'Anything's a good thing if you tell yourself often enough, right?'

Desert Storm extended a chunky hand. 'Man I feel like an asshole, we haven't even told you our *names*. Brian – Brian Harrington Junior, but don't bother with the Junior or the Harrington and if we get along, call me what everyone at home calls me – Sherman.'

'As in tank?'

'As in tank, Aussie guy.'

The tall one was Andrew and the other, still snapping away, Todd.

Andrew set the leaf down and stared, with a kind of blank curiosity, at the blank back of a calendar on the wall. I'd turned the calendar around, two, three days after arriving. The teacher I'd replaced had been crossing off the days like a jail-bird. Whatever I had to do to make this work, I'd said to myself, I would not do that.

'So why'd you turn the calendar around?' Andrew gave me a quietly provocative sort of a look. 'Some kind of mystic loner symbolism?'

Brian addressed him. 'How do you even know it's a calendar?'

'What else could it be, Professor Brian?'

'Could be his secret plan to photograph North Korea's nukes.'

Todd spoke up. 'Don't think the North exactly *hide* their munitions, Brian. I think they kinda *want* the world to know.'

Brian bristled. 'Todd. If I want advice on military stuff, I don't need it from an *artiste*.'

Andrew waited for his answer to the calendar inquiry.

I shrugged, said I'd done it to remind myself not to grind, to live in the present.

'Right,' he said, 'embrace the now. Feel the abundance. Thought maybe you were losing your mind out here. Conversations with the walls, mashed-potato sculptures, Close Encounters of the Korean Backwater Kind.'

I stared at him. He didn't seem to notice. Things felt strange, already. The word backwater had changed the air. Like any town, it had its constraints. But it had lots to like – and not just a mountain. The people who lived and worked here were generous and warm.

'Man.' Todd turned the baby-lens to the calendar. 'I wanna turn it right way round but I'm not game to lay a finger – it's like a Ouija board, I'd like, hex myself for like, all time.'

I ripped open a pack of chocolate almonds I'd bought especially for the occasion, shook them into the noodle bowl with the illustrated dragon.

'Dude.' Brian eyeballed the calendar. 'How come you didn't just like, pitch the damn thing in the goddamn trash?'

'Question,' Andrew said. 'How hard is it to get pussy round here?'

The river under the bridge was depleting. Summer had been uncommonly dry, so I'd been told.

'How hard for who, mate?' I said, disliking my weak, curtly evasive, frankly bullshit words, almost as much as his.

'For you, me – anybody who wants some.'

'Yeah, you got a girlfriend?' asked Todd. 'In Seoul, you'd be beating them away with a stick.'

'Beats beating off,' said Andrew.

Brian joined in. 'No he'd need, like, a light sabre. Not that I'm attracted to you and that goes for us all – we're definitely into women only. We're definitely not ready to go back to the States when our contracts are up. We're not too happy with how American women treated us all our lives.'

Todd seconded the motion.

Andrew waited for his answer.

From the track that wound to the mountain, Brian looked down at a woman pulling spinach. 'Some of these locals look like they've been working the same exact task since like, 1922, they're so damn stooped they don't even need to bend over to pick the greens.'

'Ask one nicely,' said Andrew. 'I'm sure one'll bend over for a handsome man like you, Brian.'

Todd aimed the tiny lens at the mountain. 'Ominous hunk of mountain-rock awaits, check.'

We came level, soon enough, with the temple. The youngest monk watched our approach. Often, I'd pass here, and he'd be shelling peas or pulling stems off a huge pile of spinach-leaves, or pegging out underwear. We must've nodded hello fifty times, without a word. It was like we had an understanding.

Brian regarded the temple. 'So are we like, going in or what?'

'We'd need to ask, or make plans in advance,' I said unsure, never having been in, 'far as I know it's not open to the public.'

'Let's ask.' With a little hop Brian adjusted the little bag on his back. 'Let's get fed.'

Todd made a face. 'Way too early for lentils.'

The monk clobbered the gong.

'Kick ass!' Brian dug the vibrations. 'I want one of those for my class.'

'Make him an offer,' said Andrew.

'Probably get it for nix,' said Todd, 'the guy can't find the money for a pair of Levis.'

'True,' said Andrew. 'His negotiating position is weak.'

The monk reservedly returned Todd's wave.

Todd aimed the camera. 'Check, mysterious temple guy. Footnote – I would not dig his gig.'

'Yeah, like no sex,' said Brian. 'Like, ever.'

Andrew slapped my shoulder. 'Like this guy.'

I let it slide – Mr Pragmatic. Mr Don't Rock The Boat.

Brian crouched at the bamboo pipe perpetually dispensing mountain water. 'Can we like, drink this?'

'No, Professor Brian, you cannot drink this water.' Todd photographed the pipe. 'It's strictly for washing the monk's SUV. And he gets mad as hell.'

'Could be sacred water, asshole.'

'Explain the cups on hooks, double asshole.'

'Relax, relax.' Me, counselling others, if my ears didn't deceive, to unwind, 'it's for anyone thirsty.'

All drank.

Andrew stared at an old lady toiling in a field. 'Wonder if she gives good head.'

I gave him a look, and said ... zilch. The woman wiped her brow; glanced in our direction. Brian waved. A downy crane glided over her, gangly and geometrical. She could have stretched and maybe touched a wing. I'd never even seen a crane this side of the bridge – neither had she, judging by her pleasantly surprised reaction.

'Check.' Todd took his pic. 'Dignified old lady, graceful bird – check. Waiting on lotus flower floating on stream – stand by for mountain.'

A rug of tiny, pinkish, fleshy leaves rustled and crunched under eight soles.

'Snakes seem to have all vanished,' I said.

'Hold up, Aussie guy,' said Todd. 'Did you say *snakes* and if so, kindly elaborate.'

'Yeah,' said Andrew. 'Now's a good time for snake detail.'

'Bring 'em on.' Brian laughed. 'Barbequed rattler!'

Summer had brought snakes – luminous lime and lurid liquorice pink whipping startled off the track. The kids in my classes told me they were deadly, but every time I saw one, all but a whisper of fear dissolved in childish thrall.

Brian chewed his cinnamon gum. 'So where do these snakes hang?'

'Smack in the middle of the trail, or off to the side, anywhere it's sunny. When it's this overcast we're probably safe.'

'That sun is super-weird,' Brian squinted. 'It's like invisible but I'm totally sweating bullets here.'

Todd agreed. 'It looks like a torch-head under a blanket.'

'Wow,' said Andrew, 'a metaphor.'

'Think it's a simile,' I put in.

Brian said, 'Doesn't a simile have to rhyme?'

'No that's a rhyme, Brian.' Andrew's measured stride had something of the military.

Todd was already breathing hard.

Talk turned, inevitably, to teaching, and I was surprised to learn they taught just three classes a day with no evenings. Suddenly I felt heroically durable, indestructible.

'And you?' Brian unscrewed the cap from his Captain America drink-bottle. 'How many classes?'

'Five, sometimes six, when I got here I just did whatever, taught anywhere anytime . . . anybody they told me to teach I taught . . . just went along so I wouldn't go home with my tail between my legs.'

Andrew kicked away a cone. 'Enjoying it?'

'Adults yes … Teenagers yes and no … Children less. I feel guilty drumming a foreign tongue into a six-year-old's skull.'

'Are you a teacher at home? Teaching your chosen profession?'

'No, learning on the job.' What was my profession? 'And you three?'

'Three Non-Teachers,' said Todd.

'Three happy campers, but.' Brian laughed. 'We're having a blast. Funniest thing for me – back me up here guys – is when we make them sing those lame-ass songs in the books. *Let's play baseball, let's eat hot dogs, we like hot dogs, do you like hot dogs?*'

I knew the kind of song. I'd made it a policy to only ever enforce the torture when the kids were at their absolute worst – and even then I'd feel a kind of defeated remorse; as if we'd all given up on each other.

'So what do you all do when you're in the States?'

'Engineer,' said Andrew.

'Business-grad. Check,' said Brian.

'Film-maker,' said Todd.

'Aspiring,' Andrew corrected.

'Film-maker,' Todd insisted.

Andrew sighed. 'Todd here is an *aspirant* – as opposed to *practising* – filmmaker.'

'Todd is able to speak for himself,' said Todd.

'Todd is prone to delusions of grandeur,' said Andrew.

'Andrew is prone to being an arsehole irreversibly,' said Todd.

'Irreversible asshole.' Andrew kicked away a stone. 'Is that like a detachable penis?'

'Brian is prone to being a sex God,' said Brian.

'Todd is lusted after by beauties on all continents,' said Todd.

Nothing stirred, either side of the trail. *Onul nalssi ga sim han. Today the weather is very calm.* Other than customary humidity, the day felt curiously undistinguished, as if autumn and summer had both disowned it.

Todd sweat enough for all of us. Brian, too, was feeling it.

'It gets easier soon.' The trail, even this stretch, was so much a part of my life, it hadn't occurred to me any might struggle.

There was something I planned to show them, soon, in the tableland marking halfway.

'So, how often do you do this hike?' Andrew asked.

'Often as I can.'

'Weekly?'

'The more I come up here the better I feel . . . better I feel, the more I come up here.'

Brian kicked away a stone. 'She sells seashells by the seashore.'

Up here in a storm I'd seen a sky-scraping pine crash into the arms of its neighbours. I'd seen sun and moon face off. On top, sunbaking nude, I'd experienced the elements in absolute equilibrium. On the way down one afternoon I'd run into the clearing elated and thrown up arms – with a noise like bunting flapping in a gale a hoary eagle launched from a tree as if from my own fingertips. It was the eagle I'd remember, all my days.

Brian wiped his forehead with a fistful of T-shirt. 'Ever meet anybody else up here?'

'It's odd. Locals tend not to bother much, what I can tell. A farmer sometimes walks his ox up here to keep it strong.'

'*No* way. A fucking *ox* comes hiking up here?'

'Never unsupervised.'

Andrew said, 'An ox needs its leisure-time too, I guess.'

Brian said, 'Don't the British eat ox-tail in their soup?'

Todd laughed. 'Man the food's bad in England.'

An isolated raindrop dabbed the back of my hand. 'How long were you in England, Todd?'

'Approximately three thousand and twelve hours. Four drizzly unproductive months.'

Andrew said, 'You never mentioned that before.'

Brian bent and scooped a fat pinecone, flipped it hand to hand. 'Maybe he's got something to hide – maybe he murdered somebody and prefers not to discuss it.'

'Okay, okay.' Todd raised palms. 'Confession: I orchestrated the demise of Dianna Princess of Wales. She tried breaking off our tryst … I overreacted. But that's all in the past and now I feel like I'm in a good place.'

Brian raised and pivoted a leg, baseball pitcher style, rocketed the cone between two pines. A wild turkey scampered and fled.

'Is it a bird?' said Andrew.

'Is it a plane?' said Todd.

'It's Super Weird Ass Chicken.' Brian.

I told them its name.

'*Gwong?*' Brian laughed. 'Fucking *gwong?* Are you fucking kidding me?'

Todd agreed. 'Not a name any self-respecting bird should consent to.'

'Unique to Korea and one of the oldest living birds.'
So I was told. Also, for the record, farcically shrill and
uncompromisingly lazy.

'Do they taste good?' Brian.

'Have you tried dog?' Todd.

'We all tried it,' said Brian.

'Yeah it's not bad,' said Todd.

'Pretty good in fact,' said Andrew.

'Considering it's a canine,' said Brian.

Todd laughed. 'As Koreans say, Good for Health.'

'*We like hot dogs,*' sang Brian.

'Are you vegetarian?' Andrew wanted to know.

'You seem the type who could be,' said Brian.

Todd said, 'I have a friend who's like one-hundred
per cent vegan.'

Brian said, 'Aren't they like, into witchcraft and
shit?'

'My buddy Andrea is not a witch.'

'Not that you're aware,' said Brian.

'She ride a broomstick?' asked Andrew.

Brian spat high into the forest. 'I saw a porno with a
bunch of witches. They had like, giant pentagon neck-
laces, and they were like dripping hot wax and all kinds
a wacky kinky shit.'

Andrew said, 'I think I heard of that. Wasn't it called *Andrea and Friends?*'

Todd's breathing was getting messy. 'Didn't that win Oscar for *Best Score?*'

I wondered should we rest, but we weren't too far now from the flattened clearing. "Hey. I have something cool to show you all, not long now.'

'Goddamn *right* this is cool.' Brian stood inside the ring of stacked, waist-high rocks. 'Looks like some kinda ceremony site deal, am I right? No let me guess – right here, unsuspecting teenage boys were circumcised under the moon.'

'Beheadings for crimes against kimchee,' Todd said.

'Strung up, castrated and cannibalised,' suggested Andrew.

For centuries the town had used this place to watch for Japanese boats come to wage war. The place had been manned around the clock, unbroken, for four hundred years.

'I'll be damned.' Andrew stared long distance.

Brian sprung onto the ring, surprisingly spry. 'Hey, men, I think I see a Jap boat. Look sharp.'

'Been over to Japan yet?' I said.

'We liked it enough.' Brian shielded his eyes in a silvery sunburst. 'Weren't so hot on how some of the locals looked at us.'

Another fat, solitary raindrop burst at my feet. 'Maybe they were thinking of Hiroshima.'

Todd ran a palm across the top of a stone. 'That old thing?'

'Wasn't that like last century?' Brian said. 'Like in one of the World Wars? . . . Man the view up here kicks *ma*jor ass!'

'Well,' said Andrew, 'it sure saved some Koreans asses.'

Brian said, 'Piece of Japanese ass is what I need next time we go.'

'Raw or well done?' Andrew.

'Raw, baby, raw.'

'Raw baby?' Andrew deadpanned. 'Do they eat it in plain view or is it a black market type deal?'

'Prefer to pick out mine live from the tank,' said Brian.

'So that's what they mean by water babies,' deadpanned Andrew.

Brian stepped down. 'So have you ever like slept up here? If it was me, I'd camp out like, every other night.'

'Not yet.' I squatted, balanced on the balls of my feet. A ladybird climbed the stem of a daisy. Downy fuzz filmed the stem. A baby bee no bigger than the ladybird hovered, oscillated, supplying faintest acoustics.

Brian wanted to know what would happen if I ever broke a leg up here. 'You don't even have a cell-phone. If it was me, I'd have my cell-phone.'

Andrew said, 'When did you ever *not* have your phone Brian?'

Todd was beside me. 'Andrew and Brian argue a lot about Brian's phone addiction – I prefer the net, I'm like a net monster, I'm on like every spare second. You're probably not even connected out here, right? Don't you ever feel like tearing your goddamn hair out not? I mean holy shit this is heavy-duty isolation.'

'Survived so far.'

'Cave men survived.' Andrew picked up a small stone.

'Yeah.' Todd had the camera out again, aiming at Brian. 'More to life than basic survival.'

'Don't miss TV. The net I can take or leave.'

'And companionship?' said Andrew. 'Take or leave companionship?'

'Depends what kind.'

'Think you know what kind.'

Todd took a photo of Brian's sneaker on the wall. 'Andrew sees himself as Grand Inquisitor, kind of an honorary role he assumes. Andrew the blowtorch. Kinda blows, but hey, it's his right, just ask Andrew.'

Andrew didn't bat an eyelid. 'Well thanks for showing us this," he said, "not every day a person sees a thing of this nature.'

He turned and looked at me as if had something else to say, then left it, for now. A raindrop burst on a rock.

Brian zipped up. 'Think I just ruined the life of a butterfly.'

'Can't be helped,' said Todd, giving it a shake a few metres away, 'but according to one theory, you likely just sabotaged desperately needed rainfall on a tiny patch of Third World.'

'So, Todd.' Andrew's interrogatory tone was back. 'These movies you're planning on making … What type, exactly?'

'Movies about people in distress.'

'You're making a movie about paramedics?'

'People's *inner* distress.'

'People in dinner dress?'

'Inner distress, asshole.'

'Oh. Ok. Only how would you know anything about inner distress if all you've ever known is living at home and going to college?'

'I've done other things.'

'Feel free to provide a list.'

'Feel free to screw yourself sideways.'

'Not much of an answer, Todd.'

'Not contracted to provide you one.'

'If you're planning to make a movie about inner distress, you must know something about it, though, right? I mean … Speak now or forever hold your dick.'

'Andrew,' I said, 'there's such a thing as imagination. He'll be able to *imagine* things. Added to which, he's far from a finished story.'

'For his sake let's hope.'

I picked up a leaf not much bigger than my thumbnail. 'Not everything can be accomplished in a blink. I mean – what sort of engineer doesn't appreciate that?'

'What sort of writer doesn't appreciate company?'

'Who says I don't appreciate company?'

'What kind of novel are you saving up for hiding all the way out here?' He took off his glasses, gave them a quick, efficient polish a fistful of T-shirt. 'I mean there are no women out here for you to meet. Wouldn't the story dynamics be less than, um, dynamic?'

Brian sighed. 'Point made, Andrew.'

'Problem with you artistic types is a lot of the time you're not interested enough in what makes *others* tick. That's a bad move for someone presuming to … to what? To critique human nature . . . Face it you're digging a hole for yourself out here.'

'Have you always been blessed with the ability to know everything about a person instantly?'

'No. But if we bumped into some cute Korean girls right now I'd know where to start – and you?'

Brian sighed. 'Out of line, Andrew.'

Andrew scuffed the ground, shaking his head. 'Too much time alone my man, too much time alone.'

Nothing he said was anything I hadn't said to myself, albeit in a different voice. On the other hand it was unsettling. What was motivating this guy? Was he so highly sexed he was stirred to spur strangers? Was he just unusually inquisitive? Was he only concerned? Was he a tool? In Korean life, to embarrass someone publicly, to injure their pride, was considered crass, the sign of a cold and unsophisticated nature. Koreans called this '*kabun*.' Maybe Andrew had been amassing anti-kabun, repressing urge after urge, hour after hour.

'So how long has it been?' Now the tone was falsely offhanded – the faux familiarity of a detective looking to lay bare a suspect.

'Long enough.' He wasn't telling me anything that hadn't occurred to me and I didn't see why I should lie.

'How long is long enough?'

'How long's a piece of string?'

Brian kicked away a cone. 'How much is that doggie in the window.'

'Andrew how is my body your concern?'

'All people concern me. People shouldn't hide.' He looked directly down as if he were reading from the trail. 'Whatever you're hiding from will be there when you're out of hiding. One with the right woman beats a lifetime out here with the chipmunks.'

Todd sighed. 'It's his goddamn body, Andrew, he's in charge of it.'

'Is he?'

'Who the fuck are you?' I snapped.

'He's General Andrew,' said Todd.

'*Gene*rally an asshole,' said Brian.

'Who the fuck is anyone?' Andrew shrugged, 'nobody's divine, nobody's so sacred and sensitive they should escape basic scrutiny.'

'What's that, like basic training?'

Todd laughed. 'This is Andrew's take on spontaneity. Give thanks – you could be getting Domineering, Alpha Andrew.'

'Flash forward.' Andrew's tone had some spice now. 'Picture yourself six months from now, alone with a woman you're hot on, one you're keen not to, err, let down. What's the score on that one?'

'Fuck you is the score.'

Brian twirled a pine-needle in his fingertips. 'Think we can all move on now.'

Andrew shrugged a shoulder. 'Just making conversation.'

'Feel free not to.' I picked up a pine sprig, flung it away.

'Whatever. Use it or lose it.' Andrew assumed the lead. 'Learn the hard way.'

Next to lose face was Todd. Only this time, it was my doing. In a way he was unlucky – I had an appetite for books and a memory to match. And he'd demonstrated a weakness for casual low-stakes plagiarism. The four of us had been swapping travel stories: embellishing, one-upping, passing so much fatuous noise I privately vowed to hand the mountain a written apology next time I presented. Filmmaker Todd was the only one without much of a story. Craving plaudits, he purloined a short story by an American writer, presenting it unaltered, with impressive remembered detail, as his own daredevil experience. Brian pronounced it the hands-down winning story. Even Andrew was impressed. At first I wasn't sure I should expose the lie. Given he had to live with Andrew and Brian, to lay him bare in front of them would be cold-blooded. But letting it slide would do him no favour, either.

I waited until we were alone, the others ahead out of earshot. 'Don't be embarrassed, Todd, but it's not a great idea to be doing that.'

Sweat dripped. 'Not following.'

Gently, I broke the news. I'd read Denis Johnson's *Arizona Hitchhiker*.

His pitch leapt a nervous notch. 'I have no idea what you're talking about right now.'

'Don't be embarrassed.'

'I'm *def*initely not, because I definitely did not do that.'

'It's just that it could be embarrassing if you did it somewhere ... somewhere ... less forgiving.'

'You're deflating *me* to pump your own tyres.'

'Relax . . . it stays between us . . . we're all here to learn.'

He blushed. 'I have no idea what you're doing right now.'

'Okay have it your way Todd.' I left him huffing and puffing.

Up ahead Brian and Andrew's row escalated. Snippets carried.

'Overreacting, Brian, overreacting.'

'Love it or leave it, love it or leave it.'

'We left six months ago, Brian.'

'My heart never leaves the United States of America.'

'Oh, say can you sing like Bruce Springsteen, pass the apple-pie.'

'You're getting closer, Andrew, closer with each unpatriotic word.'

Andrew said something.

'Say the word asshole.' Brian about-faced, walking backwards, eyeballing Andrew. 'Say the word.'

My legs pumped. Part of me fairly *willed* Brian to stiff-arm Andrew's chest and send him reeling – I'd clip him on the way past. And there it was, that was me: one taste of overheard hostility and I was anyone's: after all the yoga, all the shooting-star showers, all the growing young, I was still smitten for rancour.

Brian turned his back with a blustery roar, drove himself uphill. Any second he'd run right past the solitary soldier's headstone, hidden in the pines, with its half-moon and fishing boat engraving and epitaph, some kind of poem or saying I'd copied in pen and was always meaning to have translated. Part of me wanted it to keep it a mystery. It did something for me. And it was a sight I never passed up.

If they behaved at the top, I'd lead them to it on the way down.

'So how high up are we?' Andrew took in the scene. The fields in the east were spread out in a far-fetched tapestry of buttery yellow and blondish beige, and bullion, and unharvested greens. You could spy machinery, and people moving, ant-like.

I shrugged. 'It's weird. I've never even wondered.'

Brian looked very happy. 'I read that higher altitude boosts alertness like nine per cent.'

Andrew started on him again. 'Maybe you could finish one of your comic-books up here.'

'Hilarious.' Brian looked into the stony gully between our range and the next. 'Hilarious until I break your jaw out of the blue one day – then maybe not so goddamn hilarious.'

'Originality's not your strong suit, is it?'

'No but effectiveness is.'

'Did you say you're defective?'

'Andrew's bitter and twisted because . . . be*cause* ... any takers?' Brian plucked a pebble wedged between grooves in his sneaker sole, pitched it into the gully. 'No? Okay I'll take a swing. He's bitter because the love of his life not *only* jumped his best bosom-buddy's bones, she's *marrying* him. That was two years ago but Andrew thinks it's everyone's *job* to pick up the tab. Can we have the cheque now asshole?'

Andrew squatted, looked west. 'Brian has a problem, too. Isn't that right, Brian? Nobody mention The Car.'

'Great.' Todd stared at a shallow depression in the ledge. 'Let's humiliate our buddies and ourselves.' He gave me a shrug. 'Brian has a problem at home, it's true. Next time he touches down on the good old US of A he has a small matter to clear up – he's kind of embarrassed by it.'

'Brian is not embarrassed,' Brian faked a laugh.

Somewhere distant was a murmur, half a tremor, in the sky.

Todd went on. 'Brian was caught sleeping in the back of his car after a bender, visa-vis his broken heart. First time in four years he hadn't celebrated his birthday with his girlfriend.'

'Five. Bridgette and I were together five years.'

'Anyway it was hot out and I guess even hotter in the car. At least Brian thought so because he stripped and slept nude. So, Planet Earth being Planet Earth, along comes a mean nasty cop, spies Brian doing something Brian swears he wasn't.'

'*Shifted my arm. Shifted ... my ... arm.* Who the hell jerks off in his sleep?'

'Whatever. Anyway Brian left the country before Brian went to court.'

'I ... Did Not ... jerk off in my car.'

Andrew shrugged. 'So why not face up?'

'I know that *now*,' Brian spat to one side like he'd tasted something nasty, 'I know a *lot* more now.'

I shifted position. 'Everybody's done something somewhere they shouldn't have . . . maybe not that but —'

'Not with a cop shining a Dolphin torch,' said Andrew, 'but hey, look on the bright side, nobody can ever say you were never in the spotlight.'

'One more word and you're eating your goddamn kimchee through a straw.'

'Seen this movie, Brian.'

'Believe me it won't feel like a rerun.'

'Already does.'

'Get ready for a twist.'

'The cow jumped over the moon, Brian.'

'Did you say the *asshole fell over the mountain top?*'

Andrew crouched. 'Save you the trouble, Chuck Norris.' He positioned himself. The gully was only a couple of metres drop from the ledge, and he made it easily, landing on haunches. At once he began moving down the slope, making crunching, scraping sounds, disturbing the flinty white stones.

I wandered to the other end of the ledge and plonked down.

In low-slung crosswinds I'd never seen up here, all the shrubs dotting the gully were bending disparate directions. The sky, too, was turning strange. In some kind of cold front fast-lane raggedy brown clouds scudded west as if in flight from something mercurial in the atmosphere. Higher, clouds were milling in moody confusion.

At the other end of the ledge Brian dangled his bare feet, sipping water, watching the clouds piling up.

Andrew kept getting smaller.

Todd joined me, without sitting.

He said there was something he had to tell me.

'I'm not like those guys.' He toed a ruffle in the rock. 'There's someone at home who I love – someone I broke it off with, like a jerk.' Faraway, flits of lightning flirted. Todd had his back to it. 'I'm thinking about her a lot. Every time I'm all alone, every time I go for a walk and see something she'd dig, I'll kinda hear her voice … I'll like imagine her into the scene, into my life again.' He reached and touched a thorny bine rooted in the ledge's lip, kind of rubbed it between his fingers. 'Or I'll be like picturing what she's doing right now, brushing her teeth or throwing together her crazy walnut and orange salad, or locking up her bike before class. I mean she's not … not hot as in … I mean she's kind of unusual, kind of geeky.'

Pressure-clouds were pooling, circulating, making a kind of synoptic sludge.

'She reads more than any person on Earth. She just *consumes* books. Even on her bike there's a book in a pocket … She can persuade me to almost *any* point of view – sometimes she does it just to see if she *can*. I call her Dana DA, as in devil's advocate. Her big thing is canoeing – I mean I pretended to be into canoeing just to be with her.'

From behind us came a weird wind, a mistral shaking awake every sprig of pine. A whiff of wild peppercorn carried.

'When I'm with her I'm me, only not the me I thought I'd settle for – I have this like, way more emphatic identity. I'm like, who I'm meant to be.'

The gully shrubs shimmied in jittery anticipation.

'She has this mountain of curls she tries to keep under control, but I always tell her, a flame delights in its form.'

One wind came from the east. From behind came the colder swifter wind. Jumbled thunder like bricks falling sounded over the facing range.

'And she's salacious. Oh man is she salacious … She gives me this look, like she digs *me*. God I *love* her.'

Thunder skipped closer, backed off. Rumblier, more resounding thunder jumped on its tail.

'And lately I've had this – this *hunch* she's fallen for another guy. And I keep like, dreaming of them riding bikes around this lake. I'm on this wooden seat watching them go by and I can't tell if she can see me.'

'Call her, Todd.'

'Her birthday's like two Tuesdays away.'

'Fuck two Tuesdays, call her now. Borrow Brian's phone.'

'Think we're even in range? We're not in range.'

'Hey you *guys*!' Brian hollered. 'Guys check this *out!*'

Over the facing range, in echoing clouds, an eagle was doing cartwheels. Todd and I went to Brian's side.

Even with sixty, seventy metres between us and it, the wingspan was impressive. In the gully Andrew craned.

The eagle's movement was effortless but tensile.

Sometimes, at the point where it was upright, it appeared to suspend an instant, for show. Somehow the crossfire winds weren't messing with its rhythm. Inconsistent sheet lightning lit it and the land beneath and beyond.

The eagle disappeared behind the facing range.

We waited.

Thunder bumped around the mountain. The air felt hot and cold at the same time, like it had come down with fever.

The eagle reappeared riding an updraft; levitating. When it reached a high altitude, it came floating out over the gully. It folded its wings.

It dropped like a bag of wheat. At first I thought it might've spotted prey. For a split second I even imagined it was going for Andrew.

Five metres from the stones it flattened out and went gliding.

With deep steady beats it swung upward in smooth steady ascent.

A moment later it repeated the daredevil move, in the other direction.

Another eagle appeared – half the size of the first– beating its wings fast and shallow. Hyperactively it kept changing directions.

The first resumed its languid loops. The second followed, mimicking. Every so often it let out a little cry: *key, key*.

The first eagle torqued and went gliding on its back. The second gave it a try and nearly tumbled to the earth.

I remembered reading somewhere, when I was a kid, that some eagles test their young by pulling them into the sun's rays, holding them up in outstretched claws. If a fledgling flinched or cried the mother disowned it, sometimes even dropped it.

The first disappeared behind the pines again.

The fledgling stayed in view, sticking at its loops.

Across the sky came a cloud like a moving land-mass, like a continent adrift. Tearaway clouds jockeyed beneath.

A steady rumbling ran a ring around the ranges, and doubled back.

The first eagle reappeared.

It began doing something slow and angular – making broad, sharply diagonal rings, higher by just a few feet with each revolution. It spiralled up and up, raising its orbit.

A third eagle appeared. This one was the biggest. Tottering as if it was being hoisted on shaky cables, its wings were heftier. A kind of hoary gravitas accompanied each deep stroke.

The first came to its side. They drifted in synch. They rose together, and turned together. They rode the thermals, together. They fell together, and went separate ways.

The third eagle wandered closer to us. The juvenile came at it in a bullet-grey blur – leaping at the last possible instant like a kite tossed in a gust. A shrill happy cry lodged in all our ears. *Kiiiiiiiiioowwwww.*

The fledgling made a semi-circle and took aim again. Instead of jumping the target this time it dipped under. The cry carried again.

The eagles shared sunless sky. They left these brushstrokes.

Suddenly they were all in a line. First they made an S. Then the dropped and went rolling undulating all the way across the sky, like a rollercoaster in slowest motion. Brian and Todd howled in high-five. Andrew gaped.

I flinched when the thunderclap split the sky down the middle.

The temperature plunged.

Sheet lightning lit up the distant bay and towns beyond.

Raindrops patted the ledge, splattering bare feet.

The sky-dance was over. The eagles plummeted into a sea of pine.

It was incredible how fast things happened then. Sweeping rain came seething and hissing. A simultaneous perfectly vertical layer drummed rock. In the gully it jumped off Andrew's upturned palms and saturated every shrub and snaked in rivulets.

The facing range obscured.

Then it just vanished behind a solid wall of water.

The fields disappeared.

Andrew disappeared.

None of us said anything.

The ledge flooded. Concaves filled like paddle pools. Nobody moved. None of us were going anywhere.

It came in swoops, in cascades, retreating every so often and returning with reinforcements. It was incredible how much water was in the sky. It was incredible how good it felt just to be part of it.

It flogged and flayed us. It lashed out at us. It eclipsed us – we all just disappeared. Somebody was laughing. Somebody else was shouting. It left us with a last *Swoosh*, like a gargantuan prehistoric bird passing.

In a matter of seconds, the sun released. The air recast. Stones glistened all over the gully, as sparkling little rivulets coalesced. Over the facing range a rainbow started its climb, stalled, like it had forgotten something.

The eagles rose, one after the other, in a wheel.

The Dogs of Korea

The dogs of Korea are delivered in daylight on the open roads. Shuffling, peering from the pen, residue trust glistens in their frightened eyes. Every time it passes, your spirit takes a dive.

Self-interest shepherds righteousness to an outside lane. If you are to save the money you came here to save, learn how to teach English, honour your contract, become a more evolved, experienced person, you'll be seeing it again.

'Why does the West think we are bad for eating the dog?'

So asks Jeanie; Tuesday's 6:15 regular.

How to verbalize the self-evident?

You hear yourself saying that dogs are important, loyal creatures, that they give what we call '*unconditional love*' and '*solace*' to people who may not have much of either.

She frowns and asks, 'Why we cannot also eat them?'

She presses. 'Do you think the chicken and duck is cute?'

'Do I think ducks and chickens are cute? Well ...' Tapping a rhythm on the table with your four-colour pen.

'Cat's got your tongue!'

Part of you is agitated, part of you pleased by her stab at idiom.

'You are in a pickle!'

Feigning conciliation, you turn up both palms. 'Maybe we both are ... Anyway let's do our revision ... choosing adjectives.'

'Why do you not object to eating the duck and chicken and cow but you object to eating the dog?'

'I'm not asking you to agree with me.'

'But why do you not wish to discuss my hot topic?'

'Choosing adjectives ... Lets make a start, page forty-nine.'

'I think the West is hypocrite on this,' she says, with the chagrin of one whose opponent has rolled over, legs akimbo.

Two watchdogs endure a cage outside a mechanics' workshop. Their suffering couldn't be more obvious, or more invisible. One is motionless, head resigned on front paws, brutalised by interminable boredom; by anguish that won't be expelled in a cage. His partner in misery – all ribs, streaks and spiky ears – stands at attention. Somehow her pride rises above the life-sentence.

Two conditions are all they know:

1. Suicidal boredom

2. Rage

You and your adopted terrier passing by incite the latter – Happy lives chain free, hunger and abuse free. Flea-free is pushing it. At her sight they mash seething snouts and fangs and gums hard against the grill. Happy keeps her distance with an untroubled step; a lucky-charm amid the blighted.

Only when she's out of their sight will their fury abate.

In their remote silence, in fact, you detect a kind of perplexed awe.

Happy follows you to the mountain for your midday hike, and occasionally around the rice field roads at midnight.

You are not sure who adopted whom.

Like miniature clockwork she arrives at your thatched hut door as you're eating lunch. She's fond of Kraft Singles; partial to corn bread. Tuna doesn't exactly displease her.

She invites herself hiking. Frequently along the trail, having lost yourself in thought, or song, you will look over your shoulder, wondering how far behind she's fallen, or how deep into the woods she's strayed. More often she's up ahead, looking down, wagging and grinning as if to say, 'Chop, chop.'

Climbing to her own ever-ready beat, skirting an occasional snoozing snake, needing a hoist only where nature sets the bar too high, she's an elite power-to-weight endurance athlete.

At the rocky summit ledge, you fill a small concave with water and her little tongue activates.

Up here, in concord with the sun and breeze and clouds, as you watch the sky, watch the starlings in the valley, read, or dream up lesson-plans, Happy's habit is to hightail back to the woods. You allow her these unsupervised forays. But you do wonder what she does.

Just in time to head down again she reappears, frazzled, like a kid who strayed into the wrong street and met a bully.

June. Extremely hot. Somewhere not far from your bungalow a small dog warbles incessantly. Confronting the owner is suddenly irresistible. You step outside, around to the crumbly cement wall dividing your shack from the alleys. You hoist up, over.

Eccentric street design and your own poor sense of direction conspires. Locating the culpable home proves beyond you. Like a cryptic crossword, no matter which way you come at it, you finish where you started.

At four am the racket returns. In four hours you have a class to teach.

You wait.

And wait.

And spring naked from bed to flatten your nose against the flywire. '*What* … is *wrong* with you *people?*'

Four hours later, late for class and nudging the speed limit, flyaway petite orange leaves gust across the windscreen; it crosses your mind that last night may have been a bit petulant, boorish and selfish.

Driving your employer, as usual, home from his ailing English-language academy. You've done your best, but you've not been the cash-cow he covets. As an investment, he is beginning to see you may be a lemon.

He's in the front passenger seat. In the back seat, his wife, a retired music teacher, hums softly to herself— a woman of patience and harmony and generosity. How did he ever manage it? Then again he could swing anything – he operates a language school (*Let's All English*), a monthly tour party (*Let's Fun Japan*) and the local high school hall after hours (last week, a troupe of specially diminutive people doing cabaret to packed houses). While admiring his enterprise and verve (he's sixty-three), you two are not getting along of late. There have been disagreements over your hours. A month ago he even lost your passport. After you'd called the embassy and ordered a new one, he discovered the old one behind his couch and came to your door waving it like the winning Tatts numbers.

It has also come to your attention he may have some kind of old-school, not entirely lawful connections. You used to see him as eccentric. Now he seems dangerous.

What he thinks of you is another thing.

Tonight's exchange goes like this:

'Mr Patrick, now is summertime … Many Koreans eating traditional summer soup. Do you know?'

Nod in the key of faux-neutrality.

'Mr Patrick … Summertime I wanting you eating special soup. How about?'

'No, thank you.'

Pause.

'Why?'

'Thank you for your offer.'

'Why not want?'

You are being tested, again.

'Reason what?'

Tense in the guts, again.

'Mr Patrick … You are wanting to be writer, correct? I have for you idea giving. Charging not.' A joke. 'For you I offer extreme experience. Much extreme. Do you wanting?'

Just quit. It's not as if you haven't given it thought. Both of your lives would be far less acrimonious.

'Old colleague friend … Long time knowing … *Much* successful.' He makes a two-handed, palms-down, sweeping gesture. 'Number one dog-killing business all Korea.' His eyes meet yours. 'Jinju City, Mr Patrick. Your city – Number One dog-killing city all Korea.'

You're looking at the road again, blandly nodding to give the impression none of this bothers you.

'Tour giving you. Guided tour. Extreme encounter. Many dogs fight.'

Next pay, you're quitting.

'Mr Patrick if you are writer, you must accept invitation. Contract say: Employee Co-operation. Number One Important.'

Your nerves are all in one spot in your stomach.

'Why you not wanting? Why do you decline my invitation?'

And you do not trust your tongue anymore.

'Sunday for you convenient, Mr Patrick ?'

You turn to speak. She intercedes, reproaches him, in a pained tone. His response is terse. She looks out her window in distaste. She has taken a risk for you. You feel like pulling over and kissing her. *Red light!* You accelerate. All stiffen. All draw breath.

You apologise.

Princess spends her days tied to a persimmon tree. Picture a Husky pup crossed with a Dingo: compacted thighs, ripping Achilles tendons, the fuzzy pelt a kind of piss-yellow dirty auburn.

She is so convinced you are her liberator she's almost sold you on the heroic idea.

Red-letter-day arrives. You pin a note to the tree in pigeon Korean, informing her owner you have taken her hiking. Teenagers ditch their nearby soccer game to witness the spectacle. Much nervous laughter – these guys are sixteen and haven't known the simple satisfaction of a dog at their side.

Half a mile from the mountain, in charred, post-harvest fields, you unleash Princess. The boys' reaction says it all. *Crazy dog, Crazy dog!* They have never seen a dog run this way. Neither have you. She scorches the stubble in a swift smooth arc, now zigzagging, bounding, collapsing and writhing, flipping to her feet again accelerating.

On the mountain trail, at the rocky rise that leaves you scrambling gasping, she goes up on springs, bounds back down and repeats the scale.

She burrows into a thicket and ensnares herself, emerging in a pool of sun, rocking a pink-petals halo.

She revels in the ashes of a two-day cold camp-fire.

She terrifies a snake, chases a flabbergasted turkey within an inch of its leisurely life.

She spies an eagle in the mast of a pine and leaps marlin-like, twisting, wringing every sinew – convinced she can access the great-unmoved bird.

From the summit she views dwarfed fields and high-ways, and the sea, and glances up as if to say, 'Where to now, boss?'

Just off the track leading to the mountain, shrouded in bamboo, is a business enterprise in the shape of two large sheds. In your first months, whenever you passed, you had the blinkers on. Then one morning you heard a man thrashing at something and muted cries.

A swarthy man in pressed overalls is often at the bottom of the driveway, repairing wooden cages, wielding a yellow-handled hammer.

Something charges the space between you; something outside language. He rejects your cultural conceit with the same wordless surety you reject his cruelty.

Returning from the mountain one glary mid-morning, instead of passing him by, you stop.

He hammers away without ado. The clean, cold air vibrates, trembles with each blow.

Turning your back to him you overlook the paddies where two old women work, sharing a joke.

The hammering stops.

He stands, brushes his overalls, goes to his truck, opens the creaky driver's door and finds his cigarettes.

Six or seven feet away, he crouches on the dew, surveys the paddies. You wonder if he worked there as a teenager, if his parents worked there – or still do.

Every few moments, pressing his top front teeth to his tongue and gently inhaling, he emits an odd little squeak. One moment the noise feels malignant and the next, blameless as a baby bird. He turns his head, spits on the grass, just a little too close to your feet. Your stomach knots. Do you stay put or turn and walk away? Murmur invective in your own tongue, or greet him in your best Korean? Hard-bitten eyes meet yours. He would eat you for lunch and you both know it.

Through the bamboo comes the sound of a dog nosing a plastic bowl or container around concrete, trying, by the sounds, to winkle a last morsel. Another dog butts in. A muffled fight breaks out, degenerates. Garbled dogs rip at each other rolling and scrambling in muted uproar.

The man waits until they've exhausted themselves.

He stands, goes to the truck, unhooks a bamboo rod from the panel and turns for the path.

And you, well-trained denizen, are on your way.

Language-learning game time with your favourite high school class. Their mission, should they accept, is to offer suggestions in English, about a scene you have sketched on the left side of the blackboard. On the right side you will write their explanations, exactly as spoken. Everybody will then attempt to improve the grammar. If all goes well you'll follow up by advancing the vocabulary.

Today you do something self-defeating. Of all the scenes you could invent for this game, you choose a boy searching for his lost dog. For five long minutes, there's silence most uncharacteristic. They have no interest in the game today and appear even to resent it. Nobody has any suggestions what might have happened to the dog. No '*Dog going park play golf.*' No '*Dog go river for swimming with girlfriend dog.*'

Routed by their mystifying silence, you take up the blackboard duster.

The willowy, spectacled extrovert has his hand raised. 'Teacher, may I offer suggestion. Maybe … boy look in dog farm.'

All but the really merciful are watching you with distrust– they think you're trying to embarrass them.

Crimson, you turn your back, rub the board, a little too spotless, pick up the chalk and go blank. You wish to convey somehow that you would never double-cross them like that, that it was an innocent accident and that you owe your livelihood to them.

You glance at the clock and tell them, to their collective distress, to open *Let's All Sing*, page 12 – 'The Baseball & Hot Dogs Song'. As if what just went down was their fault.

Shin Ton Yang, Wednesday nights, soft-spoken but frank. Lessons have never felt forced and you took a liking to each other from the first. Tonight you enquire about the supposed aphrodisiac properties of dog meat.

He says, after thought, that he does not believe in it but one of his brothers favours the theory. 'He says it is very good for stamina.'

You ask if he thinks it could be true.

He thinks. 'We are all very different, aren't we?' Dextrously rotating a pen between pointer and forefinger, he adds that his brother has been known to exaggerate his prowess at other pursuits – golf, hiking, reverse parking, and drying clothes in mildly inclement weather, to name but four.

Shin Ton Yang asks if you would like to try a bowl of dog soup with him after the lesson.

You tell him you would be delighted to go out for another kind of Korean dish.

He doesn't appear to take offence. Like so many here, his pragmatic side is honed, but you wonder if he's a little disappointed in you.

You ask what his other, younger brother believes.

He says his younger brother is not interested in sex. Both of you observe a moment's silence. Beneath the window a half-hearted honk, in unhurried rush hour.

He touches the bridge of his glasses, says most of his friends agree that aphrodisiacs are probably all in our heads. You teach him the term '*placebo effect*'. With customary mellow diligence, he writes it down.

'I think eating dog ... Very bad.' She rifles through her maroon pencil case. 'Korean men ... Strange.' She pronounces it *stranjee*. She makes a note of your correction and pronounces the word afresh. So many students say *stranjee*, you've started to adopt the word yourself. Every day, you're more aware just how wonderfully *stranjee* your life is becoming here.

'I think …' Sharpening a pinkish purple pencil. 'I think dogs … Very loyal to owner. Not matter if you are rich or poor … They are always friends. Eating friends …Very…' She laughs, hand to mouth. 'Eating friends very not good.'

'Do you have to eat it at home?'

'Me not tasting.' Waving a palm. 'Brother enjoy eating with father … But mother … Not like cooking dog.'

For months this girl wouldn't look at you, during her lesson. You're not sure when or why, but something unlocked. Last week she told you that her father cuts his toenails watching TV. Last night she told you that her mother is tight-fisted – even her mother's best friend thinks so. You taught her *'thrifty'* and *'pennywise'*.

'So, then, what does your mother say when he asks her to cook dog? Do they argue about this?'

'Mother says … cooking dogs …' She pulls the dictionary close.

She learns *'unpleasant'*, *'medieval'* and *'dubious'*.

Imagine you have lived a year at the foot of a mountain.

Imagine you have two dogs for hiking companions. Let's say the smaller just gave birth to nine and won't be climbing anything for a time.

Imagine you are leaving the country in two days, after which time, the bigger dog will be sold off for slaughter. Let's say you overheard her lawful owner telling someone exactly that, in the native tongue, of which you have acquired just enough.

Let's give the scene some scope now.

You are hiking with her one last time. You are trying to imagine a way to frighten and banish her, in the lean hope she emerges somewhere to safety.

If you offer to pay the dog's owner the same sum he will fetch by selling her, he'll probably accept your money, only to sell her off once you're gone. But shouldn't you at least give him a chance? Haven't you been teaching yourself, these months, to put some faith in people? Or why not buy her and find her a new owner, in the next forty-eight hours?

The trail is ending. She's galloping parallel. Six legs leap the lichen-coated log – her bound rising from yours, yours from hers.

On the stony ledge for which you have come to feel something more than affiliation, a boy and grandfather are finishing lunch. The dog deviates to the woods, for a wander. The boy is already standing, intrigued by its autonomous trajectory.

Already, you have it in your head he will adopt. Already you have it the old man will agree to the idea.

Breathing hard letting your bag down, subsiding to frigid rock, you nod to the old timer, nod to the startled boy. You need to offer them the dog with gestures just as simple. You would like to do something fit to round out a fable.

All this is purest fantasy of course.

You are far from the trail where a dog bounded free, leaping fallen trunks, pausing for native scents, bewildered at far-flung sounds.

When
Almost
In Rome

I'd slept the dreamless sleep of a mummy, the first real sleep since making the phone-calls, two days ago.

A gleaming lobby hummed.

Passing a polished mirror behind reception I caught my unmarred reflection: a veneer nothing to do with the shock and shame and sorrow beneath. Soundless as a ghost I passed through a succinct lounge, to a quiet bar, and let my bag down on plush carpet the same crimson worn by an altar-boy in a music-video I'd once seen as a kid – a dangerously gloomy number called Do You Really Want To Live Forever, whose none-too-cheery chorus the lad mouthed standing in front of gothic candelabras. The song's abnormal message had unsettled me: how could anyone, anywhere, not want to live forever?

Sitting on a softly yielding barstool, I asked a willowy, lukewarm bartender for lemonade. I was twenty-four and still wanted to live forever, but now understood it might not be an easy thing to do.

Beside me a scrubbed, bespectacled Californian with a cherry tomato bleeding on a salad fork spoke in feather-soft tones to a stubbled man with a mug like Nasty Canasta, sitting with hefty back to the wall.

The bartender passed me a small olive-green can under a neat, frosted, upturned glass. *Limonata*.

It was lovely and cold and bitter. Lemon bits surfaced, pirouetting, somersaulting: 4-star lemonade. Last night I'd taken the only available room close to the airport. An hour from now I'd be on another plane.

I fell, again, into a deep daze, in shellshock. My first love was in a psychiatric hospital. Six weeks ago she'd been admitted. Six months ago I'd broken her heart.

She was lost. Lost in a nightmare the details of which I was having trouble even comprehending. The details didn't matter. What mattered was that right this moment she was suffering. Right this moment all I needed was to help her, show her how much I cared about her and how I still loved her. I was certain I could help her. I was certain only I could help her.

Dabbing neat, cherubic lips the American turned, asked where I was from.

'Australia.'

He touched fingertips to his ear. 'Scandinavia?'

The other said in baritone, 'Does he look like from Scandinavia?' He sounded South American, maybe Argentinian. Meaty hands made unlikely kangaroo paws. 'He say Australia.'

'Australia?' The American sparkled. 'Been there, nice clean country, clean and friendly. Laid back.'

'Young country,' I heard myself, meaningless.

The South American knocked ash from a cigarette smelling of clove and, inexplicably, horse. With a ruby-garlanded finger he scratched a peek of hairy belly between two shirt buttons. The smell of his cologne carried a hint of mint.

I told the American I'd spent a few weeks in Chicago.

'Windy City,' he said, 'love it.' The smile was uncommonly warm.

I told him how much I'd liked it, without telling him what I'd remember it for: wondering why her number kept ringing out. Wondering if she'd gotten over a rocky patch she'd been going through. Calling a mutual, truthful friend, and listening. And then asking to have the entire story slowly repeated. Nights and days since, I'd been somewhere out of time – ruinously sad without relief. It was grief without a glimmer of light; just a tidal wave of sorrow. As if my soul – the soul she'd woken and given form and seen into – was being dragged out raw and defaced. Every drop of that feeling was for her, not for me.

One more flight now: one more leg. At home I'd do anything to resuscitate everything innocent and good in our past and banish the grotesque hallucination passing itself off as the present.

The American pricked a tomato. 'See anywhere else?'

I mentioned New York. Saw myself in a shower with a buxom Czech woman . . .

'I'm jumpy in New York,' he said, 'lived there once. Told she's almost safe now but I'm not so sure.'

I felt it again – an aching, pulsing, stabbing need to be with her now.

I asked him what line of work were they in?

'Movies.' He laid his fork down, hushed. 'Finance side.'

'Which movies?'

'Which movies have I financed?'

I nodded.

'Recently?'

Kept nodding.

'Blockbuster movies?'

'Any. Big, small, past, present.'

'Familiar with a movie released oh, five years ago, starred an actress Sharon Stone? Erotic-suspense, villain uses an ice-pick and silk scarf – *Basic Instinct*.'

'Sure, pretty much everyone saw it.'

'Sure did, movie made a lot of money and made a studio sit up take note again.' He brushed petite immaculately clean hands. 'Happen to remember a house in that movie – house where, ah, Sharon Stone stays? Overlooks the Pacific Ocean? That's my house.' The smile was self-effacing, boyishly bright. 'Original locale had problems, so I offered. Scene took two days – thought I'd never get my damn house back.' He flipped to the South American. 'Made a lot of dough – we should do another *Basic Instinct*.'

'Didn't they all die, in the end?' I ventured, 'I mean, wouldn't it be difficult to resurrect?'

'Never is difficult.' The South American ground his cigarette, waved the other hand as if at a fly. 'Whenever there is sex, the people ...'

'Every obstacle a stepping stone,' said the American.

The South American lifted both shoulders. 'World is hungry for sex.'

'And *terror*.' The American nodded as if his partner had hit the nail. 'People *wanna* be terrified – we made some *real* terrifying movies, right? Made six of those, ah, Jason movies.' Clicking his thumb and middle finger. 'Villain wears a hockey mask.'

'Eight,' the other corrected. 'Eight chapter.'

'Eight?' The American grinned as if he'd gotten away with a crime nobody had ever found a name for. 'Eight beats six.'

The South American made a dull stabbing motion. '*Friday Thirteen.*'

'*Friday Thirteenth*, right, eight parts, maybe we'll shoot for double figures.'

I asked if they worked much with screenwriters.

'Temperamental, badgering, always demanding a say – so pedantic with endings, so sensitive when scenes are excised in the project's overall interest – my advice to rookie writers is take business classes on the side.' He winked. 'Am I talking to a writer?'

I felt my head shake, faintly and astonishingly, twice, in denial.

The American went back to work on his salad. I sipped. It occurred to me they may not be who they claimed to be. They sounded real enough. And strange things happened when you were overseas. Strange things happened at home, too, apparently, when you were overseas. I flashed on an image of her waking scared in the dark.

The South American burped quietly, looked at the glittering cityscape of bottles, each with its own hue and intrigue.

The bartender yawned, slipped hands into pockets, leant against the wall.

One in three made a full recovery, her doctor had told me, when I'd managed to make contact.

One in three scared me. But it also gave hope. If anybody could come out of it, she could.

I shook my head hard – a thing I must've done a hundred times. Part of me was still expecting to wake in deepest everlasting relief.

In twenty hours I'd be home. I'd *see* her. Jesus. How could –

'Attorney friend of mine knew a Missouri girl.' Softly the American spoke up. 'She went down to, ah, Australia, honeymooning with her second husband. River cruise, hundred degrees, wants to cool off. Strips down to her underwear and dives right into the river. Now, when an alligator grabs hold it does like so.' He clamped his own torso and twisted. 'Drag you deep down, roll you over and over, store you under a log like a frozen dinner – believe it? And in Australia you have these killer water wasps, electric-blue with toxic tenta-cles, only . . . now get this . . . these guys are in*vis*ible, creep around like the poltergeists of the ocean. Spotters in the choppers can't even see em. Even the birds are big and crazy in your country. Take the emu, legs as long as a fully-grown Japanese man.' The American told me about Australia's landmass being less affected than other parts of Earth when the dinosaurs cleared out. 'Just imagine the heat on that asteroid. Now there's a day the shit hit the fan.' He sought the bartender's eye, raised an uneasy pinkie. Polishing a glass, the bartender was in his own world. 'Oh, bartender … Iced water – iced, please, thank you, sorry to trouble.' He regarded me afresh; proceeded with caution. 'Heading home?'

Another nod. 'And you?'

'Asked to finance a couple of movies here, romantic comedies are good business here. Italians are a little high strung but they adore romantic comedies and I adore Italy.' The bartender put the iced water in front of him, swiped the empty salad plate, plucked a ringing phone off a black perch on the wall, gave two identical replies and replaced the receiver.

The South American ordered double scotch.

The American furrowed. 'So early?'

'For you is early.' He shrugged his heft. 'For me is okay. These European managers will always like to be keeping us waiting, waiting. They think more wait mean more money automatic.'

'One time,' the American's smile turned bashful, 'yours truly was dumb enough to drink in broad daylight, in Vegas. I mean – of all the locations. Only time I ever touched a drink in the light of day. Can't say I liked the feeling. But there's some fun in Vegas.' He glanced at the other. 'Or even Mexico City or Bueno Aries, right?'

'Anywhere is good time. Everything is inside your head.' The South American touched his left temple. 'Nobody can run from his own head.'

The American chuckled and raised his glass to me. 'Here's to never seeing a man who can run from his own head.'

The South American reached for his double. 'Some men hear trouble and suddenly they are running and hiding their heads like the ostrich.'

'No ostriches in this Roman tavern.' The American gave me another smile. 'Emu any chance?'

I made some half response. He held me with a longer, different look, as if he was trying to figure out something. The South American dragged another Marlboro out of a pack.

The American cleared his throat. 'Don't ask me who said it and don't ask me why it's just come to me. But a smart man or woman once said, "*Does he not return wisest that comes home whipt with his own follies?*"'

I made a hopeful sound, of sorts, in my throat.

He waited. 'My dad used to say a man should know when he's beat but I never believed that for one second … My dad died a lonely unknowable man. I was thirteen and I do not revere the memories he left me but I do revere the man's memory and every year on his birthday, celebrate his endeavours however misguided and disjointed. All of us face a monster some stage. Some call it master. Others go find a sword. Incomprehensible tragedy strikes? Pick up a sword, find a shield. Absolute free will does not exist and would not help us. Impassioned discipline and faith in one's abilities and in others' abilities, remember those, friend. Go to work on the monster until it can't ever go to work on you again. Be yourself, trust yourself.' He winked, held my eye.

Two Italians entered the lounge – a middle-age man in sockless, burgundy loafers and a younger man in supple leather sandals, indigo designer jeans and the loosely exalted air of one who only last night enjoyed his pick of beautiful women in a room brimming with beautiful women.

The American had dismounted. 'Ah, the late show! Good morning to you both, so nice to see you both again.'

The elder Italian made a joke about his countrymen's well-renowned disorder – screen idols and overworked agents, he pleaded, were no exception. The American wished me luck at home, as the quartet transplanted to the lounge.

The bartender watched the South American offer the Italians cigarettes. The agent said something the American found amusing. Draping one leg over the other the star smiled, forbearingly.

'Big talk,' the bartender drummed fingers, 'big talk no tip.'

I mumbled something in the American's defence, about him having only forgotten.

'Is good day for forget everything.' The bartender sighed, looked past the lounge. 'Is good day for be outdoor, for be in love.'

Five thousand miles from her I caught a mouthful of the scent of her hair. I saw her smiling catching sight of me, lifting her bag at the bus-stop, in the maroon and white summer dress. Saw her running home through rain, head bowed. Saw her brushing her teeth and laughing. Saw her in her pale blue work uniform, before a shift, walking by the seawall, the winter sun turning her Coke reddish in places, turning her hair indigo in places . . . saw her turning away her face in tears at some thoughtless thing I'd said . . . I tipped enough for three and raised the bag.

Passing the mirror in reception I took a moment's shallow relief in a reflection – in my looks.

In the car-park's asphalt glare, squinting strangers waited for the shuttle, shifting, checking watches; sweating.

The Tarot Card Reader

My mum's Tent of Tarot Mystery offered parents some fun all their own at the 1980 St Joseph's Primary Fete.

Afternoon was expiring when she saw Lee Larson's mum standing close enough to suggest interest, and asked her if she'd like to be lucky last.

For a moment it was as if the momentous woman hadn't heard. A fly circled her, in lasso, but like a horse or cow she didn't seem to notice.

Lee Larson sighed, told her to make up her mind. As he looked at the asphalt his smile revealed and concealed, the way it did in class at odd moments.

His sandal soles slapped the asphalt as he ran from the courtyard. I ran after him.

'*Dumbo*' Lee Larson had big ears and a high, unexplainably untroubled voice. Even though he couldn't spell or subtract, he was a year older than the rest of the class. He spent his days marooned at his place by the window, daydreaming and drawing UFOs, every so often smiling inscrutably. His authorized idleness sparked resentment in one or two kids who were merely a bit slow at lessons: why couldn't the teacher just stop bothering *them* once and for all, too?

When we reached the end of the playground I stretched the hole in the wire fence and he wriggled through. We pushed through scrub and bracken, all the way down to the twinkling trickling creek. A yellow frog pushed off a slick brown rock with a neat splosh and kicked away downstream as we chased.

We chased a drop-tail lizard but that disappeared under a rock, too. When Larson picked up the rock there was only moist yellow flattened grass.

Hunting for red-back spiders we each grasped an end of a rusted corrugated iron sheet and lifted. A thousand earwigs writhed – half flooded one way, half the other.

The tent was still up, when we made it back. And for the first time all day, the curtain was fully drawn.

The only other person in the courtyard was the maintenance man, Mr Matthews, folding up the Lucky Dip table. Larson asked him for a free lucky dip. Mr Matthews winked. Larson scored plastic handcuffs with a Police Department logo. I got an Incredible Hulk keyring. The Hulk was the wrong shade of green and one of his eyeballs was wonky. When Larson began telling Mr Matthews knock-knock jokes I drifted away feigning satisfaction with the keyring.

There was no laughter, or light-heartedness, or any other sound, from inside The Tent of Tarot Mystery. The heavy silence prevented me from opening the curtain.

At last my mother spoke. She sounded like someone hoping to keep the trust of a small bird, edging close. '… always tell me another time, if you prefer … can have coffee in Main Street one day or … A sandwich somewhere you feel is more … We could even – we could even go for a walk now … along the beach before it gets dark.'

I could hear Mrs Larson breathing in and out, in the silence. Then an unhappy noise like somebody emerging from too long underwater gulping for air. And the legs of my mum's chair scraping asphalt as she stood. I opened the curtain just an inch. Mrs Larson had her face in her hands, like someone washing something stinging from her eyes. My mum held her.

Lee Larson came running towards the tent with a goofy smile. I ran to him and caught him by the arm and led him away saying I had something to show him.

We ended up at the convent, all the way over on the other side of school. The convent was out of bounds, everyone knew, but he only smiled blithely, strolling up the pigeon-crap-encrusted concrete steps. He turned the silver knob on the heavy green door, turned his smile on me, and slipped inside.

For the second time in one afternoon I followed Lee Larson.

In a cool corridor, paintings of Jesus and the Apostles lined a wall. At a high, narrow window, a moth knocked around. We tried steering the moth to the door but it wasn't interested.

'Okay moth,' said Larson, laughing with strange delight, 'stay in here with the numbskull flying nuns and see if we care.'

We bounded down the convent steps, stomachs swilling with the cordial and Tick-Toks the nuns had fed us. My new friend Lee Larson said we should we tell our mums we'd been kidnapped outside school by drug-pushers then escaped by doing karate. I said we should tell the truth because nobody in the history of the world had gotten into trouble for talking to nuns.

By the time we made it back to the courtyard we both had a stitch. A stone's throw away, outside the tent, a canary-yellow balloon passed by, touching asphalt, heading for the tall wire fence around the sports courts.

Briefly we bickered over whose mother was to blame for them taking so long. When he suggested we go climb Big Ben, I said no. He flapped his elbows, called me a chicken.

'You're not even my friend, Dumbo.' I sneered and turned away from him, to go to the tent. When I looked back he was running unfazed to Big Ben. He ran all floppy, never in a straight line long, and I felt remorseful for calling him the name.

I stopped just a few feet from the tent. A sparrow darted past my eyes snapping spotted wings.

Mrs Larson's voice carried. 'Only the one I remember, anyway – there was this boy in my class . . . we lived in the same street. Sometimes we walked home together. Anyway for some reason I trusted him and he was the one I told.'

'And did he listen?'

'He listened.'

'And then?'

'Then he never said another word to me.'

'But didn't he tell anyone?'

Mrs Larson might've shrugged.

I could feel my mum trying hard to think what to say next.

'And how many times . . . I mean once is terrible enough. But how many – would you say it happened five times?'

'More.'

'God love you, Frieda.'

'I never really thought of God or anybody else loving me much after that, Theresa.'

I turned away, wandered to the school gate, out to the roadside gravel, took to throwing pebbles at the triangular head on the SCHOOL CROSSING sign. Once I'd used up all the decent pebbles in a patch, I shifted a few feet and started all over again. Whenever a car came by I pretended not to be throwing the pebbles at the sign. Just as I was becoming bored, there came a growl down at the corner. A green hot-rod came rocketing – a long-haired teenage girl leaning out a back window shrieked and frightened a magpie off a powerline and I bolted into the school to find Lee and tell him I'd spotted drug-pushing kidnappers!

He wasn't in Big Ben. Neither was he at the creek. When I found the handcuffs fastened to the diamond-shape grills in the fence around the sports court I convinced myself that he'd been kidnapped by the drug-pushers in the hot-rod. I ran around and around searching.

Jelly-legged, I came back to the tent.

'– mustn't take the law into your hands,' my mother was saying. 'Before you go *near* that town or anywhere near either of those men you *must* go to the police.'

'Theresa . . . they don't give a rat's. To them I'm a fat slag with an overactive imagination and a chip on her shoulder. Even if they believe me it's too long ago to prove.'

'Just think what could happen ... If you found yourself alone with one or God forbid both of those men and something went terribly wrong.'

I stared at my untied shoelace.

'I'll go with you,' said my mother. 'I have a friend – tough as nails, she'll go with you and so will I.'

All four of us stopped at the corner of Joseph Avenue and Barkly Hill. A line of women on bicycles filed through the crossroads. At the front a crinkly old woman with very long silvery hair gave her bell a tinkle, smiling at Mrs Larson. Down the line, bells jingled and chimed. A freckled woman with a guitar-case strapped to her back laughed and held her arms horizontal, like wings. Downhill, the women glided. One let out an unrestrained, joyous sound, and that, too, caught on. Mrs Larson blinked. Mum gave her hand a squeeze.

We were alone on McCartan, walking a footpath beside a picket fence and overhanging tree. She stopped, and stopped me, and crouched so that her eyes were level with mine. 'Make sure you're kind to that little boy.'

'I am.' On the dimmed footpath, a mash of trodden berries gave off a sour smell. I heard myself telling her about the Larson Tap – at the steel drinking-trough outside the toilets, some kids wouldn't use the tap on the far left, even on the hottest days, with a queue.

'Make sure you drink from that tap.'

'I do.'

'Tell your friends to do the same.'

'I already do – nobody ever listens, but.'

She watched to see if I was telling the truth, or another of my fibs, and in the murk my mother embraced me.

Biography

James Hughes' debut collection, *Understanding Almost Nothing Of The World* was Runner Up in the 2019 Carmel Bird Digital Literary Award. His stories have won several Australian story writing competitions. 'The Stone, The Storm, The End of Huckleberry Finn' shortlisted in the international Bristol Short Story Prize. His poem 'The Breath in Things' short-listed for the 2014 Gregory O'Donoghue Prize, an award overseen in Cork, Ireland, considering hundreds of writers around the world. A set of poems, 'Korean Harvest', shortlisted for the Josephine Ulrich Prize. In 2013 he won The John Shaw Nielson Poetry Prize. His articles occasionally appear in *The Sydney Morning Herald*. He's lived and worked in Ireland, in Australia, South Korea, Japan and America.

About this Series

Understanding Almost Nothing of the World by James Hughes is published as part of the Spineless Wonders Smalls series of small format paperbacks released to celebrate our tenth year in publishing.

To find out about other books published in this series, go to www.shortaustralianstories.com.au

9 781925 052787